A Travesty of Justice

Thornton Cline

BLACK ROSE writing

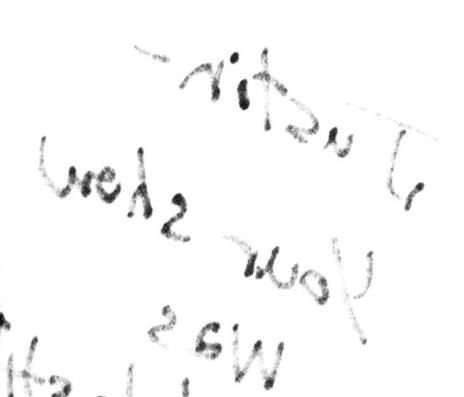

© 2016 by Thornton Cline

All rights reserved. No part of this book may be reproduced, stored in a retrieval system or transmitted in any form or by any means without the prior written permission of the publishers, except by a reviewer who may quote brief passages in a review to be printed in a newspaper, magazine or journal.

The final approval for this literary material is granted by the author.

First printing

This is a work of fiction. Names, characters, businesses, places, events and incidents are either the products of the author's imagination or used in a fictitious manner. Any resemblance to actual persons, living or dead, or actual events is purely coincidental.

ISBN: 978-1-61296-693-9
PUBLISHED BY BLACK ROSE WRITING
www.blackrosewriting.com

Printed in the United States of America
Suggested retail price $15.95

A Travesty of Justice is printed in Book Antiqua

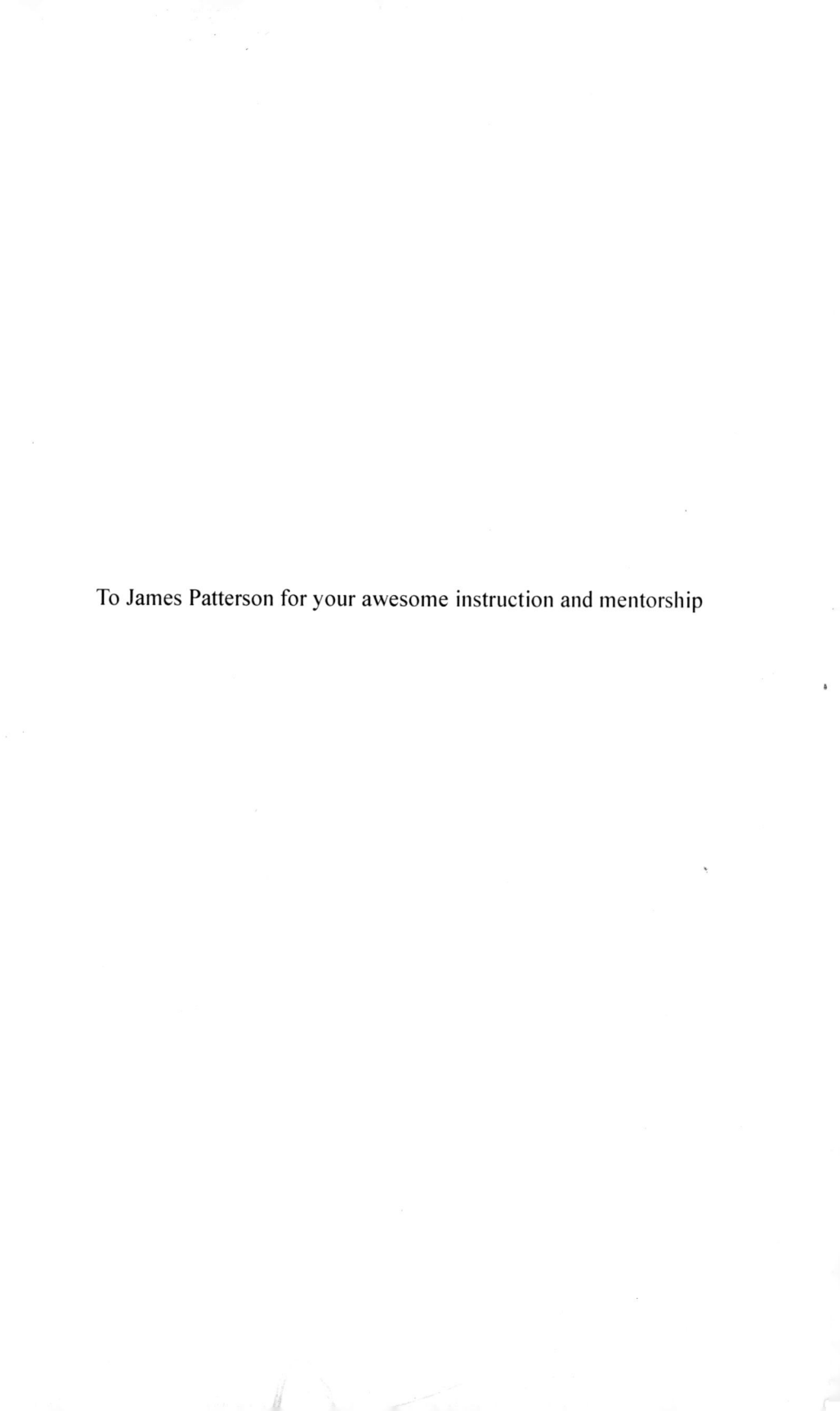

To James Patterson for your awesome instruction and mentorship

A Travesty of Justice

CHAPTER ONE

JANUARY 18, 2010 5:12 p.m.

West Omaha, Nebraska

The 911 call came from a frantic and distraught caller.

"911, what's your emergency?" the operator asked.

"I heard a loud gunshot. I think someone's been hurt or killed, I was walking the dog in the neighborhood, help, please help," the caller said as he rushed through his words.

"Slow down, stay calm, and tell me the address," the operator commanded.

"I'm, I'm at 396 Seymour Lane," the caller said as he tried to catch his breath.

"Okay, emergency vehicles are on the way. Sir, stay calm and tell me your name."

"I'm Charles Talley. I live next door to the house where I heard the gun go off. I'm worried about my neighbor, Pastor Hershel. He's inside the house and could be seriously injured."

"Officers and emergency vehicles are on the way," the operator said.

"Are you alright, Mr. Talley?"

"Yes, thank you, but I'm worried about my neighbor. It's quiet now, and the lights are on."

"Do you see anyone inside or anything suspicious?"

"No, not that I can tell."

"Ok, stay calm, we are only a few blocks away."

Charles could hear the wailing of the sirens in the distance as they grew closer.

All at once, flashing blue lights appeared over the horizon of

A Travesty of Justice

the street.

First, the police cars arrived, and then the ambulance and fire trucks all quickly pulled up to the curb of 396 Seymour Lane.

"Is this the house?" an officer asked.

"Yes," Charles replied.

The officers and paramedics rushed up the steps to the front door. The officers rang the doorbell and knocked on the door repeatedly. There was no answer.

"This is the police, open the door," the officers shouted.

There was no answer, only silence. An officer jiggled the door handle.

"It's locked, sir," he reported.

The officers drew their pistols as the others kicked the door down.

They rushed into the house pointing their weapons in all directions. The officers searched the living room, kitchen, and dining room but found nothing.

They slowly climbed the stairs of the two-story house with their guns pointed ready to fire.

Once the officers reached the top of the stairs, they turned and carefully walked the long hallway with their weapons pointed in all directions. They turned right and swiftly opened the bedroom door.

As they entered the bedroom, their eyes opened wide with alarm as they took it all in. To the right of them beside the bed was a man slumped against the wall soaked in a pool of blood. Beside his right hand was a .38 caliber pistol lying on the floor. To the left above the body were blood stains seeping down the wall still fresh from a crime that had occurred less than an hour ago. There were pieces of grey matter from the brains still intact on the wall and floor where he lay.

There was no sign of life in his body. The paramedics were careful not to disturb the body. The police took photos and wrapped the bedroom with yellow tape, which read POLICE LINE: DO NOT CROSS.

Soon the television and news reporters arrived on the scene.

They were asking questions of the neighbors and prying—looking for anything they could find that would give them a lead in the story.

The Omaha CSI team rushed to the scene and began collecting evidence. A tall, broad-shouldered, neatly dressed detective in a sports coat and tie began questioning the neighbors searching for possible witnesses.

"Are you Charles Talley?" the detective asked.

"Yes, I'm Charles Talley."

"I'm Detective Calhoun of the homicide division of the Omaha P.D.," he said as he reached out to shake Mr. Talley's hand.

"Where exactly do you live?" Detective Calhoun asked.

"I live next door at 394 Seymour Lane," he replied.

"Can you tell me what happened?" the detective asked.

"I was walking my dog just before dinner when I passed the Pastor's house and suddenly heard a loud gunshot."

"Were the lights on when you heard the gunshot sound?"

"Yes, sir, the lights have been on ever since you all got here."

"Did you see anything suspicious?" the detective asked.

"No."

"Did you see any suspicious people or cars in the neighborhood?"

"No, sir."

"How long have you known your pastor friend?"

"He's been our neighbor for well over 15 years. Everyone loves him. They call him Pastor Hershel."

"So you're saying he didn't have any enemies?" the detective asked.

"Not that I know of. He's been pastor of the First Church of God for years. He has quite a following. He is adored and loved by everyone."

"Do you think he would kill himself?" the detective asked.

"Absolutely not. He's a man of God. He had too much going for him. He also knew the consequences of what would happen to him if he had committed suicide. Suicide was definitely not an option."

"I read where he lost his wife not too long ago," the detective replied.

"Yes, that is true. He mourned for her for quite a while. He still misses her, but he would never commit suicide."

"They found a gun beside him with his fingerprints on it."

"That might be true, but I know Pastor Hershel. He would never kill himself. He had too much to look forward to. Did they find a suicide note?" Talley asked.

"We haven't found one yet," the detective replied.

"Don't you think that's kind of strange, no suicide note?"

"Many people who kill themselves leave suicide notes, but not everyone. Maybe he was too embarrassed to admit it."

"Or maybe he didn't do it," Talley interrupted the detective. "I'm not about to tell you how to do your job detective, but if I were a betting man, I would say someone killed him."

"What makes you think that Mr. Talley?"

"Pastor Hershel would never kill himself. And as far as I know, Pastor Hershel never owned a gun."

"We are running a trace on the gun as we speak. We'll find out whose gun it is."

"I just think it is awfully suspicious that the Pastor didn't own a gun and that he was found dead with one next to him."

"If he didn't kill himself then who do you think would have done it?" the detective asked.

"With all due respect, sir, that's for you and the Omaha Police Department to find out."

"If indeed anyone did kill the pastor," the detective interrupted him.

There was a pause of silence from Mr. Talley.

"We did find something unusual in his house," the detective said.

"What's that?" Mr. Talley asked.

"We found a couple grams of cocaine in a plastic bag in his room," the detective said.

"So now you're telling me the pastor is a drug addict?" Mr. Talley replied.

"No, I'm not saying that. It looks suspicious that he had a

few grams of coke lying around in his room."

"I could never see the pastor doing or selling drugs. It's just not in his character. That is so unlike him."

"Well, sometimes we think we know a person well, and then we find out something about them that they've been hiding," the detective said.

"No, it's just not Pastor Hershel. There is something mighty suspicious going on. Again, if I were a betting man, I would say Pastor Hershel was murdered, and the gun and drugs were planted to make it look like the pastor was a desperate man who took his own life."

"Well, whatever the case might be, we will uncover the truth—suicide or not," the detective said. "Thank you for your time, Mr. Talley. We will be in touch with you should we need any further questions answered."

Detective Calhoun finished taking notes on his tablet and walked into the crime scene area for one final look. As he scoured the perimeters of the pastor's house something caught his eye. He noticed reflections of strange footprints left on the beige tile in the kitchen. It was if someone had tracked mud into the pastor's house. The mud was still fresh from the newly-fallen rain that had sprinkled the ground only a few hours earlier. There was one set of tracks that entered the back door to the kitchen and another set of tracks that exited the back door. It seemed rather strange to the detective. Detective Calhoun began to examine the tracks further and discovered a few of the footprints on the light brown carpet that led to the stairs which led to Pastor Hershel's room.

"The prints look like a size 14 boot imprint. That is some tall guy," the detective said.

"Get a photo of that would you?" Detective Calhoun asked the CSI team.

"This might not be a suicide after all. Looks like someone tried to frame the pastor but got a little sloppy," the detective said.

"Right now, at this point, I'm calling this a homicide, so we best be looking for the killer."

CHAPTER TWO

JANUARY 19, 2010 7:45 A. M.

Methodist Hospital, Omaha, Nebraska

"Sir, sir, wakeup," a woman's voice spoke loudly to me as I lay in my hospital bed.

I slowly opened my eyes and focused on a blurry face smiling at me.

"Where are my glasses? I need my glasses," I said.

"Here they are, Mr. Green," the female voice said.

I reached for my glasses and placed them over my nose and ears.

"Now that's better," I said.

To the side of my bed stood a tall, brunette woman dressed in light blue scrubs. She was smiling at me.

"Let's fix your bed so you can sit up. They brought some delicious eggs, bacon, toast, and orange juice for you," she said as she raised my bed and adjusted my pillow behind me.

"But first let's check your blood pressure and heart rate," she said as she placed her stethoscope on my chest directly over my heart.

"Mr. Green, your heart is beating strong and sounds good." She placed the tray of food on my bedstand.

"I'll let you eat, but I'll be back soon."

I took a few bites of the egg and bacon. I couldn't eat much. It was hospital food. Since I had awakened from my coma two weeks ago, I had about all the hospital food I could stand. It made me long for my sweet wife, Samantha, and all of her amazing recipes that she could turn into unforgettable tasty meals.

God, I really miss her, my dear Samantha. I sure wish she was here today.

But then my heart and mind came back to Earth again, and I realized that she had been gone for five years and there was nothing I could do about it except go on with my life.

My thoughts were interrupted when the same nurse greeted me again.

"How was your breakfast, Mr. Green?"

"Not bad. But it's not even close to how great a breakfast my late wife would make."

"The food's that bad, huh?"

I shook my head up and down with a definite yes.

"Well, Mr. Green, we need to talk about something that just happened to one of your family members."

"Who is it, what happened?"

I was interrupted by a middle-aged man who stepped into my room all dressed in a black shirt with a white rectangular collar in the center of his shirt collar area. He resembled one of the Methodist pastors who I used to know back when I was going to church.

"Mr. Green, I'm Pastor Newman, Chaplin for the Methodist Hospital here," he said as he extended his hand toward me to shake mine. He was soft spoken with his words. He wasn't smiling, and at that point I knew there was some bad news I would have to face.

"Okay, Pastor, tell me the news," I said.

He pulled up a chair and sat next to me. The pastor looked directly at me with his solemn eyes.

"Yesterday, sometime around 5 p.m., your brother-in-law Hershel went to be with Jesus in Heaven."

"You're talking about Hershel; the one I know?"

"Yes, the one who was married to your late sister."

There was a long pause of silence as I searched for words to say.

"God, that's so sad. What happened to him?"

"He was found slumped over on his bedroom floor lying in

A Travesty of Justice

a pool of his own blood."

"Was it an accident?"

"They found a gun that apparently fell out of his hand when he pulled the trigger."

"Are you saying he killed himself, like as in committing suicide?"

"It appears that way."

"But that's not the Hershel I know. He would never kill himself."

"I'm sorry, Mr. Green. I'm not here to judge him or your family. The police are investigating it. And they may well discover that it was a homicide. But for now they are looking at it like Hershel committed suicide, as hard as that is to take."

"I wonder why I haven't heard from my son about Hershel?"

"Maybe he's busy with work."

"He lives right here in this town. It seems like he would know what's going on. I'm going to have some words with him. He should be keeping me informed on family matters. In fact, I haven't seen Norris since I've been in this hospital. That's just not like him. He always calls. But I haven't received one call or visit. Something's wrong."

"Well, I'm sorry I can't help you with your son, Mr. Green. He's probably like my son. He gets really busy with his work and forgets to call or visit for a long time. I don't like it, but I have learned to accept it, it is what it is," Pastor Newman said.

"Could I offer a prayer for you, Mr. Green?"

"You mean right here, right now?"

"Yes, right here, right now."

I laughed nervously and said, "Thanks, but I think I will pass. I'm a private person and don't like to air out all of my laundry to just anyone."

"I'll try not to take your remark personally. I was offering if you felt like you needed some prayer."

There was complete silence.

"Okay, Mr. Green, have a wonderful day. I wish I had better news to tell you. But I can tell you this much—God loves you and he is definitely in control, whether you think so or not."

Pastor Newman stood from his chair, shook my hand, and closed the door behind him.

Then the phone in my room rang. I fumbled with the wires and cords to reach it. I picked it up and said, "Hello?"

"Is this Mr. Green?"

"It depends, who's asking?"

"This is Captain Willis of the Omaha Police Department. As soon as you are released from the hospital, we need to talk."

"About what?"

"We are investigating the attempted murder of you. And we've got some questions to ask."

"Okay, I don't know how I can help you."

"We need you to come down to the station as soon as possible."

"Okay, I will. You can count on that."

"Thank you, Mr. Green. We'll talk soon," Captain Willis said as he hung up.

How much of what I remembered after my coma could be true? I need to talk to Norris and catch up.

I lowered my bed into the resting position to take a nap. I was worn out. This all could wait until later as I slipped off until a deep sleep.

CHAPTER THREE

CONTACT LOST

"Good morning, Mr. Green. I'm here to check your vitals," the cheerful voice said.

I reached for my glasses on the stand beside my hospital bed and placed them over my nose and ears. I focused my eyes on a petite and pretty red-haired woman dressed in blue scrubs with a stethoscope draped from her neck. She gave me a big smile.

"I'm feeling fairly good today. I can't wait to get out of this place. They tell me I've been in here for almost six weeks.

It feels like I've been here forever, but I don't remember being here for six weeks," I said perplexed.

"That's because you were in a coma for almost a month, Mr. Green. That's why you can't remember."

"The last thing I remember before I got here was dangling from a building exit fire ladder outside in an alley, being shot, and falling to the ground in my own pool of blood."

"That's right, Mr. Green. They tell me you were life-flighted to Cedars-Sinai Medical Center in Los Angeles. You were in a coma, but as your vital signs improved, you were flown to this hospital in Omaha where you remained in a coma for 28 days."

"Who had me flown and admitted to this hospital?" I asked.

"I don't know, perhaps a family member," she replied.

"I wish I knew who sent me here. It was probably my son.

Speaking of my son, have there been any calls for me today, yesterday, or any time since I've been here?"

"Let me check. I'll call down to the front desk. They keep a log of all incoming calls and messages."

The nurse picked up the phone and called the front desk

receptionist.

"This is Nurse Talley in room 712. Could you please check the call and message log to see if there have been any calls for Mr. Louis Green since December 14?"

She paused for the reply.

"Okay, I'll wait."

Nurse Talley quietly rested the phone on her shoulder.

"Mr. Green, they've put me on hold. I should know something in a few minutes."

After what seemed like the longest time of waiting, Nurse Talley finally asked, "Are you still there?"

She waited for the reply.

"Oh, okay…so you're saying there haven't been any calls or messages for Mr. Green except for the one yesterday from Captain Willis of the Omaha Police Department. How strange. Well, thank you for checking," she said as she hung up the phone.

"There you have it, Mr. Green. If you were listening to my conversation, the receptionist said there haven't been any calls or messages for you during your stay here."

"How could that be?"

"I don't know, but the only person who called was Captain Willis of the Omaha Police Department. He called yesterday."

"I can't believe that my own son hasn't at least called or stopped by to see me. That is so unlike him. I'm worried that something is wrong."

"I'm sorry, Mr. Green. Life gets really busy sometimes, and we forget to do the important things that we intend to do."

"But we've been growing closer lately, and we'd been talking more than ever. I just don't understand it."

"I'll leave you alone, Mr. Green. Let me check your heart before I go."

She placed her stethoscope over my chest and listened carefully.

"Your heart's beating a little fast today, but it sounds healthy and strong. I think your fast heartbeat rate is due to you being anxious about your son not calling."

A Travesty of Justice

"You're damn right, I am. Where's my cell phone?"

"When you're admitted into this hospital, they store all of your valuables in a safe until you are released."

"So how am I supposed to call my son?"

Nurse Talley reached over to my phone on the bedstand and handed it to me.

"Do you know your son's number?"

"Yes, that's one thing I do remember."

I dialed his number and waited.

"You have reached the voice mail of Norris Green. You know the drill. Leave me a message," the voice said on the other end.

"Son, this is Dad. I've been trying to call you. Where are you? I'm here in room 712 at Methodist Hospital. I miss you. I haven't heard from you in ages. I'm getting worried about you."

I hung up.

"Damn, I can't get him on the phone."

"He's probably at work," Nurse Talley said.

"He answers his text messages. But I can't send him a one, could you do me a special favor?" I pleaded.

"If you think you can sweet talk me into sneaking your cell phone out of the safe, you can't. I could get fired if I did it and they found out."

"Well, no harm in asking."

"I feel your frustration and wish I could help you. Have you tried your son's wife? Do you know her number?"

"I sure do."

I dialed my daughter-in-law Julie's number and waited.

"Hi, Julie, this is Louis. I'm trying to reach Norris. I haven't heard from him in six weeks. I'm getting worried. I'm in room 712 in Methodist Hospital. Please call me back ASAP."

"Okay, there you go, no answer from either one of them. How strange. What would you do if you were me?"

"I'd keep trying until I reached them. All you can do right now is wait for them to call you back. I'm so sorry, Mr. Green, I've got some other patients to look after. I'll stop by and check on you later. Maybe you will have heard from one of them by then."

"I think I'll try one more number. I know Norris's work number, and maybe I can reach him there at the law firm."

I dialed the number of Norris's work. I waited.

"Seymour, Smith, and Trousdale, how may I help you?"

"This is Louis Green, and I am trying to reach my son, Norris."

"I'm sorry, sir, he no longer works here."

"What do you mean he doesn't work for you anymore? What happened to him? Is there someone I can talk to about this?"

"I'll connect you with Joel Seymour. Maybe he can help you."

"Thank you," I said as I waited for Mr. Seymour to answer.

"Joel Seymour speaking."

"Mr. Seymour, this is Louis Green, Norris Green's dad. I heard that my son no longer works for your company."

"Hello, Mr. Green. Yes, it is strange what happened. It was about six weeks ago. He didn't show for work. We called him, left messages, and tried to call his wife. Neither one of them returned our calls. He missed several important cases where he was supposed to be representing clients. We tried our best, but we can't deal with unprofessionalism of just not showing up for work."

"Hadn't you considered the possibility that maybe something was drastically wrong considering how dedicated and committed Norris has been to his work?"

"Yes, we did. But we can't meddle into our employees' lives."

"I wish you had called me to let me know of Norris's strange disappearance."

"I'm sorry, Mr. Green, but we don't intrude into others' lives."

"Now I've heard it all. Do you know how upset I am at you and the company for not notifying me?"

"I am sure you are upset, sir. We hope Norris is alright and wish him the best."

"That's all you can say, 'you wish him the best?' We're talking about someone's life here."

"Well, Mr. Green, it is unfortunate what happened. But I must go, I've got some clients who need me right now. Goodbye."

Mr. Seymour hung up the phone. I was still fuming from the law firm not notifying me that my son was no longer with the company. I was way past worried and didn't know exactly what to do.

I was emotionally drained from the uncertainty of the whereabouts of my son. I was growing anxious about a lot of things: when I was going to be released from this hospital, finding my son and family, Hershel's death, and having to talk to the police about my attempted murder. I tucked my pillow under my head and drifted to sleep for another nap. I promised myself that tomorrow would be a brighter day.

CHAPTER FOUR

THE UNKNOWN

"Good morning, Mr. Green. Did you sleep well?" Nurse Talley asked as she opened my hospital room door.

"Not really. I was restless all night. I couldn't get to sleep."

"Is it about your son?"

"Yes, I am beyond worried. I'm sick about it."

"Is there something you want to talk about?"

"Yes, I called my son and daughter-in-law and left messages. I still haven't heard from them. It's been over six weeks since I've had any communication with them. The last time I remember talking to Norris was when I was in California just before I went on the *After Hours Show* with Chris Callahan."

"Wow, that has been a long time."

"You're telling me. He hasn't once visited me or called since I've been admitted to this hospital."

"I'm sorry, Mr. Green. I'm sure you're frustrated."

"What's really strange is that I called his work yesterday. I talked to Mr. Seymour, one of the partners in the firm. He claimed that my son hadn't been at work in over six weeks. Can you believe that?"

"You mean he went AWOL?"

"Yes, they say that he never even called. He disappeared, and they haven't heard from him or his wife since then."

"That's strange."

"You're right, particularly since he's the most dedicated and committed worker I've ever seen. He has a deep passion for his work. He's proud of what he does."

"Bizarre."

"What hurts the most is that he didn't keep me in the loop, and the company he works for didn't bother to call to let me know he had been missing."

"Corporations for you."

"Yeah, you're right. Mr. Seymour said that they don't meddle into their employees' personal lives."

"Unbelievable. You tried calling your son's wife, right?"

"Yes, and no answer or return calls."

"What about calling her at work?"

"That's a great idea. In fact, I know the number to the children's hospital where she works."

"Mr. Green, you've got an amazing memory for someone who has been in a coma for 28 days. Maybe you can get some answers from them at her work."

"Great. Thank you. I will try her now." I reached for the phone by my bedstand.

I dialed the number. It rang.

"Children's Hospital and Medical Center," the voice said.

"Yes, I am trying to reach Dr. Julie Green, please."

"One moment, I'll connect you."

"This is Dr. Murphy speaking."

"Dr. Murphy, I'm Louis Green, father-in-law of Dr. Julie Green. I'm trying to reach her. It's urgent that I get ahold of her."

"I don't know what to tell you, Mr. Green. It is very strange. She's been working at this hospital for over 10 years, and then one day she doesn't show for work. It's not like her. She's dedicated and committed to her patients and to this hospital. Her patients keep asking me when she will be in."

"When is the last time you've seen her?"

"Gosh, it's been well over six weeks."

All at once, a wave of chills ran through my body. My heart felt like it had stopped when I heard Dr. Murphy say she hadn't been around in over six weeks.

"Her husband, Norris, has disappeared too. I called his law firm, and they said he hasn't shown for work in over six weeks."

"I'm so sorry, Mr. Green. I hope you'll find them. Here's my number: 402-573-6757. If you hear any news about Dr. Green, please call me."

"I will call you if I hear anything. You can reach me here in room 712 at Methodist Hospital."

"Thank you, Dr. Murphy," I said as I hung up the phone.

"Nurse Talley, I'm really scared about my son and daughter-in-law."

"I know, I heard."

"I think it's time to take action."

"Are you thinking what I'm thinking?"

"I'm going to call the police and file a missing persons report."

"That's the best thing you can do right now."

"When do you think I'll be released from this hospital?"

"If it was up to me, I'd release you today. You have improved tremendously. You are about ready to be discharged. We are waiting on Dr. Turney. He has the final say. I expect him to arrive sometime in the next hour or so."

"Nothing personal, Nurse Talley, but it would be awesome to get out of here."

"No worries, Mr. Green. I'd feel the same way if I'd been here as long as you have."

"Nurse Talley, could you please help me look up the Omaha Police Department number?"

"Why certainly, Mr. Green."

She searched her smart phone for the number.

"Here it is: 402-672-5000."

I picked up the phone and dialed the number as she read it to me. I waited.

"Omaha Police Department, may I help you?"

"I would like to file a missing persons report."

"One moment, I'll connect you with that department," the receptionist said.

"Detective Williams speaking," the voice said.

"I would like to file a missing persons report," I said.

"What is your name and contact number?"

"My name is Louis Green. I am currently in Methodist Hospital in room 712. I will probably be discharged tomorrow morning."

"Are you a resident of Omaha?"

"No, I live in Griswold, Iowa. I am visiting."

"What's the name of the person missing?"

"There are two people missing right now. There could be two others missing, too. They are Norris Green who is my son, and Julie Green who is my daughter-in-law."

"Do they live in Omaha? If so, what is their address?"

"2126 Cedar Point Road."

"Did you say there could be others missing?"

"Yes, their two children, Sadie who is nine years old, and Michael who is four."

"How long have they been missing?"

"About six weeks."

"And you're just reporting it now?"

"I've been in Methodist Hospital with a coma for 28 days and am still recuperating. The receptionist at the main desk says that they haven't heard from my son or daughter-in-law since I've been here. I've called and left messages with both of them. I haven't received any messages or returned calls."

"That doesn't necessarily mean that they are missing."

"I called my son's work and they said he hadn't shown in six weeks. The same thing happened when I called my daughter-in-law's work, the Children's Hospital and Medical Center. They said they tried to reach her and she hadn't called them back."

"That is strange. It does sound suspicious."

"You're telling me. I am worried and frustrated."

"Okay, I'll go ahead and start the process of filing a missing persons report on the two of them. I will need some more information, and I will need you to come down to the police station to fill out an official report."

"It looks like they will be discharging me tomorrow from Methodist. I will be sure to stop by and get the report filled out."

"Thank you," I said as I hung up.

"Nurse Talley, you are an answer to prayer. You have helped."

"That is sweet of you, Louis. I wish you the best of luck on finding your son and daughter-in-law. I need to go and take care of some of my other patients. I will see you later, sweetie," she said as she left the room.

I lay in bed anxiously awaiting Dr. Turney's visit. He would hopefully approve my release from this hospital, and I could take care of some urgent, neglected business that had been knawing at me. Tomorrow couldn't have come soon enough.

My hospital door opened and in came Dr. Turney, all smiling with cheerful-looking eyes.

"I've got great news for you, Mr. Green. I am discharging you tomorrow at 10 a.m. You will be free to go. You have improved greatly since you were first admitted. Your therapy has been very beneficial. Your brain injuries have healed. Your vitals are all strong. All of your functions have returned to normal. Bottom line is that you can walk out of this hospital tomorrow a free man."

"Thank you, Dr. Turney. Nothing personal, but I can't wait to get out of this hospital."

"I fully understand how you feel. Good luck with everything, Mr. Green," he said as he shut the door behind him.

CHAPTER FIVE

A FREE BUT DISTRAUGHT MAN

10 a.m. couldn't have come any sooner. It was Thursday morning, and I was ready to celebrate my newfound freedom. Dr. Turney had given his okay for my discharge from the hospital, and now it was time for me to pack. I found a bag of my clothes — the clothes I had worn when I was first life-flighted to Cedars-Sinai Medical Center in Los Angeles. Apparently, the clothes were delivered to Methodist Hospital when I was transported again from Los Angeles to Omaha.

I tore off my hospital gown and slipped into my boxer shorts, undershirt, pants and shirt. I slipped my feet into some socks and shoes. I took a look at myself in the bathroom mirror. I combed my hair and smiled at myself in the mirror.

I told myself, "This is a new day Louis. Everything's going to be okay."

Nurse Talley opened the door of my hospital room.

"You're sure looking spiffy today. Are you ready to taste your newfound freedom?"

"I sure am. Thanks for all you have done. I feel like a new man."

"Mr. Green, we'll walk with you if you'd like to the main desk, so you can pick up your valuables."

"Thanks, but no thanks. I'll do it on my own."

"Okay then, I'll phone down to the main desk and let them know that you're on your way."

As I began to open the hospital door to leave, Nurse Talley reached out and gave me a big, warm hug. I reciprocated.

It felt good to know someone genuinely cared about me.

"Thanks again, Nurse Talley," I said as I began walking to the elevator.

I took the elevator to the ground floor and headed to the main desk. When I arrived at the main desk, there was a friendly, heavy-set woman who greeted me with a large smile.

"Are you Mr. Green by any chance?"

"Yes, I am."

"Would you please sign here by your name and date it?"

"Okay, there."

"Here's your bag of valuables. Please check to make sure everything is in there."

I opened the plastic bag and found my wallet. I looked through my wallet and was amazed to see that I still had almost half of the cash left that I had received from my Social Security check I had cashed the day I was a victim of the Bank of Omaha robbery-hostage incident. All of my credit cards, my Iowa driver's license, and Social Security card were still in my wallet. I found my shiny silver watch, my truck keys, and my cell phone.

"Yep, everything's there. Thank you so much. Hey, would you be able to call a cab for me please?"

"Certainly, Mr. Green."

She picked up the phone and dialed the number.

"I need a taxi for Mr. Louis Green at the front entrance of Methodist Hospital, please."

There was pause.

"Great, thank you, sir," she said as she hung up the phone. "Mr. Green, just follow the signs that point to the front entrance. Wait outside by the benches. A taxi should be there in five minutes."

"Thank you, ma'am."

I followed the signs that pointed to the front entrance.

The anticipation of being free from my over six weeks of hospitals was overwhelming. I felt like I was free of everything. I took the automatic double doors which led to the outside. It was a beautiful sunny day but chilly for January. I could see my breath as I inhaled and exhaled. I was alive. I had survived the

A Travesty of Justice

gunshot wound to my brain on that gory night when I was chased by my killer back in December.

Now I've got to find Norris, Julie and my grandkids. That's my number one priority.

Without warning, a bright yellow cab pulled up to the curb of the front entrance. A short, stocky man stepped out.

"Are you Mr. Green?"

"Yes, I'm alive and well."

"Where do you want to go?"

"Take me to 2126 Cedar Point Road."

"You've got it," the cab driver said as he helped me into the back seat of the cab and closed the door.

The driver pulled away from the curb and turned right into the street traffic.

"It's a cold day today," he said trying to start a conversation.

"But the sun is shining, and I'm alive and free."

"That must be a good feeling."

"It is after being in two hospitals for the past six weeks."

"Two hospitals in six weeks. What for?"

"It's a long story."

"Well, we've got about 10 minutes before we're there. Give me the short version."

"I was in L.A. on December 7 recording the *After Hours Show.*"

"Excuse me, but did you say you were a guest on the *After Hours Show*?"

"Yes, that's what I said."

"What for?"

"After surviving a bank robbery-hostage incident that happened at the Bank of Omaha."

"Wait a minute, aren't you *America's Hero*, Louis Green, the one who's been on every news channel on the planet?"

"Yes, that's me, and I don't know that I've been on every news channel on the planet."

"Wow, you're famous."

"I don't know if I'd say I'm famous, but life has been pretty crazy for me since that bank robber-hostage incident."

"Well, go on with the story."

"After the show, a security officer walked me to the curb to get a taxi. When the taxi pulled up, someone came out of nowhere and shot the security guard in the face. I ran for my life toward some buildings. The gunman chased me down several alleys. I tried to escape, but I ended up reaching for a fire exit ladder. There I was dangling from the ladder. Next thing I know, I had been shot in the head. I landed in my own pool of blood."

"That's scary. But, here you are alive to tell the story."

"They tell me at the hospital that I was life-flighted to Cedars-Sinai Hospital in Los Angeles. Then they transported me to Methodist Hospital shortly after that. I was in a coma for 28 days."

"Wow, that's an amazing story," the driver said.

"Yes, and I'm still standing, alive and well. Right now, I'm headed to my son's house at 2126 Cedar Point Road. I haven't heard from him in over six weeks. He hasn't called, and he didn't come to visit me while I was in the hospital."

"What do you think is up with that?" the driver asked.

"I don't know what to make of it. It is strange. It's not like him. We always talk on the phone. I've called and left messages but haven't heard from him. What's even stranger is that I called his work and he hasn't worked for his company in over six weeks."

"Are you saying he quit?"

"No, I'm saying he never showed up for work six weeks ago. There were no explanations."

"Sounds like something's wrong."

"You're telling me. I am paying a surprise visit to my son's house. I need to find out what's going on."

"We're here. That will be $42.00, sir."

I handed him a fifty-dollar bill and told him to keep the change.

I closed the cab door behind me as I climbed the long elevated driveway toward the front door. Every light in the house was on, which I thought was strange since it was

A Travesty of Justice

daylight. There in the driveway were their two cars.

What are they doing home on a Thursday?

I stepped up to the stained-glass front door and rang the doorbell. No answer. Then I pounded my fist against the door a bunch of times, but there was still no answer.

I shouted so loud that I'm sure someone in the neighborhood heard me.

"Norris, Julie answer the door. It's me Louis. Someone answer the door."

Still there was no answer. So I walked around to the back and peered into the windows. It was quiet and still. I didn't see any signs of anyone in the house.

How strange.

I jiggled the back door and suddenly it opened. I stepped inside the kitchen area and shouted, "Norris, Julie, Sadie, Michael, it's me Louis!"

It was eerie. The house was quiet and still. I looked around the kitchen and noticed that there were dirty dishes sitting in the sink. There was cooked food still sitting on the burners of the stove. The stove burners were fortunately turned off. There were clusters of flies and gnats everywhere. I stepped into the dining room and my eyes protruded out of my sockets.

The dining room table was set with utensils and plates.

There was uneaten food on each plate—molded chicken, molded green beans and potatoes. Each glass was filled with water, milk, or tea. There were flies and gnats feasting on the uneaten food, which appeared to have been sitting on the table for a good while. There was a strong stench coming from the dried food on plates. It appeared as though the family had prepared to eat their dinner and were interrupted by something or someone.

Icy cold chills ran through my body at the thought of possibly finding their wounded dead bodies somewhere in the house. But I found no one. I took the steps to the upstairs bedrooms. I opened Norris and Julie's bedroom door and noticed something strange. Julie's designer purse was resting on their bed. I peered inside and found money in her wallet with her credit cards and driver's license.

Nothing's adding up here. Julie never leaves her house without her purse. Why would the whole family suddenly leave their food on the table when they had prepared to eat dinner?

I opened the door to Sadie's bedroom. There was no one around. A quick check of Michael's bedroom revealed the same scenario—everyone was gone. I searched every room and closet in the house. The Green family had literally vanished—not a trace of them. Panic ran through my whole body. I took a walk around their property to see if I could find a trace of them or of any bodies.

There was no trace. I checked the mailbox and it emptied the box of mail and an official-looking note from the U. S. Postal Service fell out. It was dated December 21, 2010 and read: PLEASE BE ADVISED THAT YOU WILL NEED TO PICK UP YOUR MAIL AT THE LOCAL U. S. POST OFFICE. THERE WILL BE NO FURTHER DELIVERY TO THIS RESIDENCE. I figured that the reason the official note was left was because the mailbox was full and couldn't hold anymore mail.

I called Detective Williams of the Omaha P.D. from my cell phone.

"This is Louis Green. I called yesterday to report two missing people."

"Yes, I remember, I talked to you."

"Well, now there are four people who are missing."

"Who are the other two?"

"Sadie Green who is age 9, and Michael Green, age 4. They are the children of Norris and Julie Green."

"How long have they been missing?"

"For over six weeks."

"Six weeks and you're just reporting it now?"

"I didn't know they were missing until yesterday. I've been in Methodist Hospital for over five weeks and was in a coma for 28 days."

"I'm sorry, Mr. Green, and I do understand."

"How soon can you get down here to the police station? I need you to fill out an official missing persons report."

A Travesty of Justice

"If I can get a cab quickly, I can be there in less than 30 minutes. What's the address?"

"We are at 505 South 15th Street."

"Thank you, Detective Williams. See you soon," I said as I hung up the phone.

I could see it was going to be a long day, and I was going to spend a long time in the police station. But I had to find my son and daughter-in-law, and if that's what it would take, I was ready.

CHAPTER SIX

THE POLICE REPORT

The cab pulled up in Norris and Julie's driveway. I hurried to get in as the driver got out, greeted me and helped me into the back seat.

"Where are you going?" the driver asked.

"Take me to 505 South 15th Street, the Omaha Police Department."

"Yes, sir, I'm on it. We'll be there in 20 minutes."

"What a cold day," the driver said. "Are you from around here?"

"No, I live in Griswold, Iowa."

"What brings you here?"

"It's a long story. I first came to visit my son and daughter-in-law for Thanksgiving about nine weeks ago.

Then all of this bad stuff happened to me and my family.

It was like we had all been under a curse. I went back home to Griswold and then flew to Los Angeles. Next thing you know, I found myself here in Methodist Hospital with a coma where I had been admitted over five weeks ago."

"Wow, that's a lot of coming and going for that amount of time."

"You can say that again. And now I'm headed to the police station to file a missing persons report for four people in my family: my son, my daughter-in-law, their nine-year-old daughter, and their four-year-old son."

"Seriously?"

"Yes, seriously."

"I am sorry sir, but how can a whole family be missing?"

"That is what I'm trying to find out."

"The strange part is that neither my son nor daughter-in-law showed for work over six weeks ago. And I stopped by their house less than an hour ago to check on them. No one answered the door so I finally jiggled the back door and it opened. I called for them to answer, but it was still and quiet. Both of their cars are parked in the driveway."

"Maybe they went on a vacation."

"That's not likely since they didn't notify their work. And the strangest part is that there are dishes piled in the sink. There is food still on the stove burners and in the dining room, the table is all set for them to eat. That doesn't make any sense."

"Wow, you're right, it doesn't make sense."

"It doesn't, does it?"

"I don't want to scare you, sir, but is it possible they could have been kidnapped?"

"You mean abducted?"

"Yes, abducted."

"It's possible. That's such a scary thought."

"Who would do such a thing. Do they have any enemies?"

"They don't, but I do."

"You have enemies?"

"Oh, yes, one enemy who put me in the hospital with a coma."

"Seriously?"

"Yes, seriously. His name is T. Bone Jones. He is a very dangerous fugitive who escaped from the Nebraska State Penitentiary.

"I saw his photo all over the news back in December. I think he is still on the loose. Why would a fugitive want to kill you, sir?"

"Revenge."

"For what?"

"T. Bone Jones was one of the five masked men apprehended for the November 30th Bank of Omaha robbery-hostage incident that was all over the news."

"Oh, I remember now. Aren't you *America's Hero*, Louis

Green?"

"Yes, that's what they call me."

Before we could talk any further, the cab pulled up in front of the Omaha Police Department.

"Here we are, Mr. Green. I wish I could hear more of the story you were telling me. But we both have got to go."

"Thank you for the lift."

"Oh, that will be $43.00," the driver said.

"Here's a fifty. Keep the change," I said as the driver helped me out of the back seat.

"Good luck with finding your family."

"Thank you," I replied and turned to climb the steps to the front entrance of the police station.

I opened the front door of the police station and was greeted by an officer at the front desk.

"May I help you, sir?"

"I talked to Detective Williams about filing a missing persons report. He asked me to meet with him today."

"Why yes, I remember speaking to you on the phone earlier. You must be Louis Green."

"I am."

"Well, have a seat over there while I get him."

"Thank you," I said as I took a seat in the waiting area.

Panic returned to my body just thinking about the whereabouts of my son and daughter-in-law.

Could they still be alive? And if so, are they being held against their will? Are they being held for ransom money?

I also thought that it was possible the police would find their bullet-ridden bodies somewhere in a field or in a dumpster.

Deep chills moved through my body just thinking those thoughts.

"Mr. Louis, Mr. Louis, I'm Detective Williams."

Detective Williams must have repeated himself several times before he got my attention.

"Oh yes, I'm sorry. I must've been dreaming. I'm Louis Green."

"Follow me to my office, Mr. Green."

A Travesty of Justice

We walked to a security door, which opened using a code entered on the wall keyboard. The large steel door closed behind us as we walked down a long hallway.

On the right was Detective Williams's office. He opened the door as we both entered.

"Have a seat. Can I get you a cup of coffee?"

"Yes, that would be great."

"What do you want in your coffee?"

"Coffee black, please."

He poured the cup and handed it to me.

"Okay, as I understand it four people are now missing. Is that right?"

"Yes, four people in my family are missing. "Norris Green, Julie Green, Sadie Green, and Michael Green."

"Is that spelled GREEN or GREENE?"

"The first one is correct."

"Okay, please give me their ages."

"Norris is 42 years old, Julie is 41, Sadie is nine, and Michael is four."

"Do you have any recent photos of them?"

"Yes, I do," I said as I reached for my wallet.

I pulled out a photo of Norris and Julie together. And then I found separate photos of Sadie and Michael, which I handed to the detective.

"Thank you. They're a good-looking family," the detective said.

"Thank you," I replied.

"Do you realize that each year in Nebraska over 300 people go missing. Only 74 of those are discovered alive and well. The others are difficult to find. It's as if they vanished into thin air. We don't give up looking for them. Sometimes it takes years before we find them. Sometimes it is best to hire a private investigator if they haven't been found in a reasonable amount of time. I want you to understand the odds we are up against each year in trying to solve these disappearances."

"I do understand how difficult it is. So let me try to help. Norris is six feet, two inches and weighs about 158 pounds. He wears his hair long with a beard. His hair color is brown. And Julie is 5 feet, 11 inches and weighs 140 pounds, I guess."

"That's very helpful, thank you. So when is the last time you saw them?"

"It was quite a while ago. December 1st was a Wednesday. That is when we had Aunt Hilda's funeral. I spent the day with Norris, Julie, Sadie and Michael. Then I drove back the very next day to Griswold, my hometown. That's the last I had seen of them. That was about two months ago. I did talk to my son, Norris, each day on the phone from Thursday, December 2 through Monday, December 7. They tell me I was found shot in a back alley in Burbank, California, on that Monday. I don't remember anything after that. They say I was life-flighted while in a coma to Cedars-Sinai Hospital in Los Angeles and then transported to Methodist Hospital here in Omaha a week later."

"Wow, you've been through hell and back."

"I'll say. The hospital staff has no record of my son or daughter-in-law visiting or calling while I was admitted. I even checked my voicemail messages on my cell phone after I was released from the hospital, and there were no messages or calls from either one of them."

"What about where they work? Have you contacted their employers?"

"Yes, as a matter of fact, Norris's law firm said that he never showed for work about six weeks ago. And he never called.

The hospital where Julie works as a pediatrician says that she never showed for work either—about six weeks ago."

"Okay, so we can put the timeline of their disappearance to somewhere between December 10 and 14."

"That sounds about right."

"Are there any friends or other family members who might know their whereabouts?"

"We have cousins and some friends, but I don't know their contact information. I can probably get that for you soon. And Uncle Hershel was found dead in his house a few days ago. Hershel would have had a lot of those contacts."

"What happened to Hershel?"

A Travesty of Justice

"He was found dead in a pool of blood with a .38 revolver lying next to his hand. The police first thought it was a suicide, but they've gathered more evidence, and it looks more like a homicide."

"Pastor of what church?"

"First Church of God here in Omaha."

"Can you think of anything else that might help us to locate your son, daughter-in-law, and grandkids?"

"Yes, as soon as I was released from the hospital, I took a cab to my son and daughter-in-law's house. I knocked and rang the front door bell. There was no answer. So I walked around to the back and knocked on the door. There was no answer. Then I jiggled the back door, and it opened on its own. I took a few steps into the kitchen. That's when I knew something was wrong. The kitchen sink was piled with filthy dishes. There was a strong stench of rotten food throughout the house."

"That is bizarre. Sounds like they left in a hurry or were abducted."

I told him how I had found Norris's wallet, Julie's purse, and both car keys left behind in their bedroom.

"That sounds very abnormal," he said.

"Yes, and how do you explain their disappearance since both of their cars were still parked in their driveway?"

"Unless someone stopped by to pick them up," the detective said.

All of a sudden there was a knock at Detective Williams's office door. A tall man with dark hair and a mustache stepped in and introduced himself.

"Sorry to interrupt you, Detective Williams, but there is an urgent matter I need to discuss with Mr. Green concerning his attempted murder. By the way, I am Captain Willis, the one you spoke with on the phone the other day."

"No worries, Captain, we were just wrapping things up," Detective Williams said.

"We've got new information on the fugitive killer, T. Bone Jones, the one who tried to take your life on December 3 and on December 7. He also killed a prison guard and critically injured another guard during the prison break at the Nebraska State Penitentiary in Lincoln on December 2.

There was sudden silence as Detective Williams and I tried to take it all in.

"We've been investigating your attempted murder in cooperation with the L. A. Police Department and with Interpol."

"Interpol, doesn't that investigate international crimes?" I asked.

"Yes, we've discovered that T. Bone Jones did not act alone when he tried to kill you. We learned that he has strong ties to the Russian mafia better known as Bratva."

"Wow, that is scary. But why would he want to kill me?"

"Well, for starters, you disrupted and broke up their gang of five when you captured them on the day of the bank robbery-hostage incident at the Bank of Omaha on November 29. That's some serious stuff—breaking up the Russian mob. Your heroic actions were responsible for putting them behind bars. They had a good thing going with their string of bank robberies and money-laundering schemes. But there's a whole lot more that we still don't know about T. Bone and his involvement with the mob. We also don't know how many more of the Bratva members are still out there."

"Why are you telling me this?"

"To let you know that you are still in serious danger. T. Bone and the mob aren't finished with you yet. You are a threat to him. You can still do a whole lot of damage to him and the mob. You need to know who you're up against. Bratva has networks all over the world in almost every country. They are also very active in the U.S. The CIA and FBI monitor them daily."

"Do you think they could be responsible for the disappearance of my son-in-law, his wife, and their children?"

"I most certainly do. And I think they could be tied to your Uncle Hershel's unfortunate death a few days ago."

"That is scary."

"Where are you staying while you are in Omaha?"

"I haven't booked a hotel yet. I was just released from

A Travesty of Justice

Methodist Hospital today."

"Okay, well, would you like some police protection?"

"I suppose."

"This is no joking matter. Mr. Green, if I were you, I would accept police protection. Don't take this lightly, this is a grave situation."

"I know, that's why I need to carry a .38 with me."

"It's going to take more than a .38 to stop T. Bone and the mob."

"Speaking of my gun, I left it back in Griswold with my truck at my farm."

"That's too bad."

"You're right. I need to buy a gun now. What do you suggest?"

"You know you've got to fill out paperwork to buy a gun. But I would recommend you get a .45 automatic pistol."

"I've never owned one, but I hear the .45 is very effective."

"Yes, the .45 automatic is very accurate in hitting your target and guarantees that you don't miss since you've got quite a few rounds to shoot."

"Thanks for the gun lesson, Captain Willis. I think I best be going now."

"Here's my card with my number. Would you call me when you check into your hotel? You are a moving target, Mr. Green. I want to make sure you are safe."

"Will do," I replied.

"Be careful out there," Captain Willis warned.

CHAPTER SEVEN

WATCHING OVER MY SHOULDERS

I was awakened the next morning by the bright sunlight piercing through the drapes in my hotel room. The clock read 9:00. I looked around and realized where I was. I wasn't staying in a hospital bed in Methodist Hospital anymore—I was a free man. I could do as I pleased, at least that's what I told myself. Here I was, alone, staying at the Days Inn on Miracle Hills Drive in Omaha. I sure missed Norris, Julie, and my grandchildren. I missed Hershel. And I longed to return to my farmhouse in Griswold. I couldn't wait to end all of this mess with my family, the murder of Hershel, and, all of those troublesome issues. It didn't seem like I had any freedom at all.

I lay in bed in my pajamas and decided to catch up on the news. I surfed the channels on the television mounted to the wall in my room. It seemed I couldn't escape the fate that was happening to me. All of a sudden, an Amber Alert flashed across the screen: AMBER ALERT, SADIE GREEN, AGE 9, AND MICHAEL GREEN, AGE 4 ARE MISSING.

The pleasant memories of my grandchildren were suddenly unhinged when their photos were shown on the screen.

The Amber Alert continued: SADIE GREEN IS FOUR FEET, EIGHT INCHES AND WEIGHS 53 POUNDS. SHE HAS CURLY LONG BLONDE HAIR WITH GREEN EYES. MICHAEL GREEN IS THREE FEET, FIVE INCHES AND WEIGHS 33 POUNDS. HE HAS SHORT BROWN HAIR WITH BROWN EYES. THEY ARE BELIEVED TO HAVE BEEN ABDUCTED FROM THEIR HOME POSSIBLY ON DECEMBER 10. FUGITIVE KILLER T. BONE JONES IS BELIEVED TO BE

A Travesty of Justice

INVOLVED IN THIS ABDUCTION. HE IS ARMED AND DANGEROUS. IF YOU HAVE SEEN THESE CHILDREN OR HAVE ANY INFORMATION, PLEASE CALL THE HOTLINE NUMBER AT 800-843-5678.

I couldn't watch the news any longer. Reality hit me. Norris, Julie, and my grandchildren were gone. My heart broke. I wept uncontrollably. I cried out to God, "Keep my family safe from harm. Help me find them, Lord."

My mind filled with horrid thoughts. I kept graphic scenes of the bodies of Norris, Julie, Sadie in a vacant field somewhere in Omaha. I had to do something and had to do it quick. I decided to buy a .45 pistol to protect myself.

I showered, shaved, and dressed in khaki pants with a blue plaid shirt. I skipped breakfast because of what I had to do.

I left my hotel room looking over my shoulder constantly, afraid there was someone hiding in the hallway ready to kill me. I walked the stairs to the first floor lobby and waited for my cab outside. The cab arrived quickly. The driver helped me into the back seat and closed the door.

"Where are you headed?" the driver asked.

"Take me to Guns Unlimited at the Sports Plaza One on 120th Street."

"You've got it, sir. Buying a gun today?" the driver asked.

"You'd better believe it."

"You look really worried. Are you in some kind of danger?"

"Yes, I'm in knee-deep danger. You could say I'm a moving target."

"That bad, huh?"

"There's a fugitive killer after me. He won't stop until I'm a dead man."

"Wow, that's scary. I'd buy a gun, too. We're almost there."

"Is it my imagination, or are we being followed? That black Tahoe has been tailing us for a good while."

"I'll cut down a side street and see if he is still following us."

We took a detour down a short side street. The Tahoe was still following us.

"You're right, that car is following us. What do we do now?"

"Well, we can go to the gun store and see what the dudes in the car do."

"Shouldn't we call the police?"

"We should if they try to make a move after we get to the gun store."

It was tense and quiet as the cab pulled up to the parking space on the street in front of the gun store.

"We're here and they're behind us, about a block up the street watching us. It looks like there are three of them in black sport coats. They appear to be very large men, but can't tell for sure. I'll wait for you here and call the police."

"Thanks, buddy. Here's the tab. Keep the change."

I hurried into Guns Unlimited and rushed to the counter. I waited as there was a customer ahead of me. I looked around my shoulder to see if anyone had followed me into the store.

Finally, the salesman waited on me.

"I need the best .45 automatic that you've got," I said.

"Are you in some kind of danger?"

"Yes, I need this gun for protection."

"Okay, here's the latest and best .45 automatic that we sell. It can fire 12 rounds quickly. It is called an HK USP .45."

"I'll take it," I said.

"Don't you want to know the price?"

"Sure," I replied.

"It will cost you $849 plus tax."

"I'll take it."

"Here, fill out the 4473 form. It's six pages of questions from ATF."

"What is ATF?"

"It's the Federal Government requirement. It stands for the Bureau of Alcohol, Tobacco, Firearms, and Explosives. I'll need your Social Security card and driver's license."

The salesman wrote down the make, model, and serial number on the application.

I handed him my credit card, and the salesman ran a background check on me.

"You're approved. You're good to go. Here's your new .45,"

A Travesty of Justice

he said.

I smiled as I felt the power of that new gun in my hands.

"Will you need some rounds of ammo, too?"

"Yes, definitely."

"How many?"

"Enough to stop a mob."

"Oh, I see. Well, here are 48 rounds of ammo. That should do it. All you have to do is put another clip of rounds in the gun after you've fired 12 rounds."

All at once I felt safer than before knowing I had four clips of ammo available.

"Here's your credit card back. Just sign here."

"Thank you!"

As I held the gun in my hands, I loaded it with a clip of ammo. I was ready to take on the mob or anyone for that matter.

I had a renewed sense of confidence as I walked confidently to the cab that was waiting for me outside the gun store. I waved to get the attention of the cab driver who had fallen asleep, slumped down, while he waited for me. I walked around to the driver's side and tapped on the window.

"I'm ready," I said.

The driver wouldn't wake up. I looked closer and suddenly my whole body became paralyzed, struck with fear. There was blood everywhere. The dashboard, seat, and the driver's shirt were covered in blood. I panicked. I felt helpless. The driver had been shot in the back of the head several times. The engine was still running. I reached for my cell phone and called 911.

"911, what is your emergency?"

"My cab driver has been shot several times. I think he's dead. Please help, send someone here quickly," I said almost inaudibly and in a helpless panicked state.

"Slow down and take a deep breath. What is your location?"

"I'm in front of the Guns Unlimited store on Sports Plaza One, 120th Street."

"We are in route, sir. Try to stay calm."

CHAPTER EIGHT

FIVE MINUTES LATER

There were cop cars everywhere. The traffic had crawled to a stand-still as 120th Street outside of Guns Unlimited was barricaded. The paramedics arrived to the gruesome scene of the cab driver slumped over in the taxi covered in blood. His body was covered with a sheet. Yellow police tape was stretched across the barricades so no gawkers or spectators could enter.

"Your name, please," a detective asked me.

"I'm Louis Green," I mumbled still in a state of shock.

"What is your address?"

"I'm staying at the Days Inn on Miracle Hills Drive."

"Where are you from?"

"I live in Griswold, Iowa. I'm visiting."

"May I see your driver's license?"

I reached for my wallet in my back pocket and handed it to him. The detective looked it over and he studied my face several times.

"I know you, you're Louis Green, the guy on the news they call *America's Hero*."

"You've got it."

"What happened here? Could you tell me your side of the story?"

The detective listened as he took notes on his pad.

"I called a cab from Days Inn about an hour ago. The driver picked me up and took me to Guns Unlimited."

"What were you doing in Guns Unlimited?"

"I feared for my life and decided to buy a gun to protect

myself. I asked the driver to park outside the store and wait for me. When I returned to the cab, I found him slumped over against the steering wheel covered in blood. It looked like he had been shot several times in the back of the head. His engine was still running."

"Anything else?"

"Yes, when I saw that he wasn't sleeping but actually had been shot, I called 911."

"We checked to see if he'd been robbed and there was no money missing," the detective said.

"Why would anyone want to kill a cab driver other than to rob him?"

"Unless he had enemies?"

"This guy didn't seem like the kind who would have enemies."

"How's that?"

"He was the friendliest and most likeable guy I'd ever met."

"Sometimes they can fool you. Did you see anything suspicious looking?"

"Why, yes, we did. We were followed by someone driving a black Chevy Tahoe on the way to the gun store."

"How do you know you were being followed?"

"The cab driver wanted to see if we were being followed. He took a detour down another street. And sure enough, they were following us. He said that it looked like three men in the car dressed in black attire. Oh, and he said they appeared to be very large men."

"What happened next?"

"They followed us to Guns Unlimited. The cab driver said that they were parked on the same side of the street about a block away from the cab."

"That does sound suspicious."

"That's more than suspicious. I'd say they were trying to kill us both. But they got to the cab driver first."

"How do you know they did it?"

"Look, detective, first my brother-in-law is found dead in his house; my son, daughter-in-law, and their children come up missing; there is a psychopathic killer still after me, and now this cold-blooded killing of my cab driver happens, and you don't think there's any connection? You don't think those guys in the car weren't trying to kill me, too?"

"We've got to have proof, Mr. Green. We can't just go around arresting people based on your theories."

"Say what you want detective, but I'm a marked man. Those dudes following us in the black Tahoe are connected in some way to all of these incidences."

"Can you identify these men? Do you have a license plate number?"

"All I can tell you is that the men were rather large. They were dressed in black sports coats, possibly black suits. They all had dark sunglasses on. For all I know, they could be working for the CIA or FBI."

"Funny, Mr. Green, real funny. How about a license plate number?"

"I don't have a license number. I could barely see the plates at that distance. But, I would recognize the car if I saw it again."

"Why's that?" the detective asked.

"There was something peculiar about that car. It had fancy, gold-plated rims and gold-plated hub caps. The car was jacked-up in height. It seemed like it was three feet off the ground. You don't see too many cars that look like that."

"Interesting, Mr. Green, very interesting. "Those are all of the questions I have for you at this time, Mr. Green. Here's my card. I would like to talk to you further about this murder. I will contact you when I need to. Thank you, sir. Oh, by the way, I just found out that the bullets that killed your cab driver weren't from a .45 but from a .357 magnum. So, you are off the hook."

I called another cab. The driver helped me into the car, closing the back seat door.

"Where to, sir?"

"Take me to the Days Inn Hotel on Miracle Hills Drive."

I held my newly purchased friend closely in my hands. I was not about to let my new .45 automatic out of my sight. I would

A Travesty of Justice

carry it everywhere and would sleep with it if I had to. There was an enemy on the loose, perhaps a multitude of enemies after me. If I had to defend myself, I would defend myself to the very end—police protection or not.

My mind ran recklessly through all of the devastating incidences of today, yesterday, and the days before. I had to find out where Norris, Julie, and my grandchildren were and if they were still alive. I had to know who killed Hershel. I had to find out how to apprehend my psychopathic stalker who had attempted to kill me once and wanted so badly to finally kill me for good. Those thoughts weighed heavily on my mind.

I was in deep thought when I was interrupted.

"We're here at the Days Inn. That will be $39.50."

I handed the driver a fifty.

"Here, keep the change. Thank you," I said as I stepped out of the cab and headed toward the lobby door of the hotel. I took the elevator to the third floor and walked step by step down the long hallway to reach my hotel room, 322. I was beat. Today's traumatic episode of my cab driver being killed in cold blood while I was shopping for a gun made me exhausted.

I opened my hotel room and tore off my clothes. I threw them on the chair beside my bed. The clock read 6:55 p.m., but it felt much later than that. Before I prepared to go to sleep, I checked my voicemail messages on my cell phone.

There was one message for me. I listened attentively. It was from my cousin in Atlanta.

"This message is for Louis Green. Louis, this is your Cousin Janie here in Atlanta. I am so sorry for the loss of Hershel. It is such a tragedy, so very sad. My deepest condolences to you. A celebration of life service to remember Hershel is going be held at The Church of God in Omaha this Tuesday, January 26. We would be honored if you could give a tribute to Hershel."

I put my phone down, sat on the bed, and reflected for the moment. That message from Janie revived a well of past emotions and memories that I had stored deep in my heart and mind. All at once, pictures of my late sister, Hilda, with Hershel all came back to me. It was haunting to realize that I was only with them a few months ago when they were alive and well. It made me realize how precious life was and how fleeting life can be. Feelings of guilt, anger and rage overcame me.

I brushed my teeth, washed my face, and turned out the lights hoping to get a good night's rest. I was totally fried from the traumatic day and thought I could go to sleep. Instead, I lay awake thinking of all of the injustice in this world.

When I thought of Hilda and Hershel's death, how my son and daughter-in-law with their children were still missing, how there was a psychopathic killer still trying to finish me, and how my cab driver was brutally killed, a great sense of morality overcame me.

What a travesty of justice. How can they get away with this?

Even though I didn't know exactly who they were, I knew that those unknown perpetrators who had committed these heinous acts of crimes needed to be brought to justice.

I clutched my faithful new .45 automatic in my hand beside me in bed for fear of being the next victim.

Any second now T. Bone Jones or the Russian mob could kick down my door, open fire on me, and I'd be lying here dead drenched in blood.

CHAPTER NINE

UNCLE HERSHEL'S FUNERAL

Tuesday morning greeted me with bright rays of the sun piercing through my window. It seems I had forgotten to pull the shades the night before. I reached for my glasses on my night stand beside my bed. I placed them carefully over my ears and nose. I tried to focus after being in a deep sleep for some time. The clock in my hotel room read 10:02 a.m. I was so worn out from the trauma of the past week that my body succumbed to the intense emotional stress. I must have slept for over eleven hours.

As I stepped out of bed and stretched my arms and legs, my mind reminded me that today was a very special day — it was Hershel's funeral. Then I realized that I didn't have any dress clothes to wear and I had less than four hours to shop, get ready and travel to the church. All of my clothes had disappeared when I was transported from the Cedars-Sinai Hospital in Los Angeles to Methodist Hospital in Omaha. I quickly jumped into the shower and washed myself. I found the same khaki pants and a polo shirt to wear. I dressed quickly, brushed my hair and teeth, and slipped into my socks and shoes. I grabbed my jacket, cell phone, wallet, and keys. I shut the hotel room door behind me. I hurried down the hall to the elevator, took it down to the lobby, and called a cab.

It was a pretty sunny day for Omaha in January, and it looked like the temperature might reach a high of 45 degrees. The cab arrived quickly. It was a familiar face.

"Where are you headed this morning, Mr. Green?" the driver asked.

"I know you. You picked me up at Methodist Hospital about a week ago," I said.

"Good memory."

"I didn't catch your name."

"It's Al. Call me Al."

"Okay, Al, I need to go to Kohl's Department Store to get a suit."

"Which Kohl's?"

"The one closest to the First Church of God on North 24th Street."

"Yep, I know exactly where it is. That would be the one on Oak View Drive. We're on our way, Mr. Green."

"Thanks, Al."

"Dressing up for a special occasion?"

"You could say so."

"Wedding or a party?"

"Neither—a funeral."

"I'm sorry."

"Yes, me too. It's for my brother-in-law. He was the senior pastor of the Church of God. It was very tragic."

"What happened, if you don't mind me asking?"

"A little more than a week ago, Hershel was found dead from a bullet wound to his head. He was slumped over sitting in his bedroom. They found a gun beside him in a pool of his own blood. The police found cocaine in his room."

"Oh, my."

"They first thought it was a suicide. But later they discovered tracks of mud leading from the back door of the kitchen up the stairs and into his room. They are looking for a killer with large feet—size 14."

"That is very tragic. I'm sorry for your loss."

"Thanks, me too. It has been nothing but a travesty of justice since the day I set foot in this town."

"How so?" Al asked.

"I found myself mysteriously in Methodist Hospital waking up from a long coma; my son, daughter-in-law and their children have been missing for over six weeks; Hershel's been

A Travesty of Justice

killed; my cab driver was brutally murdered a few days ago while he was waiting for me to return from shopping at Guns Unlimited; and there is an investigation by the police for the attempted murder of yours truly."

"Wow, I'll say that's a travesty of justice. You must be a strong and courageous man, Mr. Green."

"I'm feeling a little more confident since I bought my faithful friend, my .45 automatic."

"You carry a .45?"

"I most certainly do."

"Wow, a .45 automatic."

"I got it about five days ago. I had to fill out some paperwork with the ATF. But when you've got a psychopathic killer and the Russian mob after you, this .45 becomes your faithful friend."

"You can say that. You're a brave man, Mr. Green."

The cab driver turned into a shopping center and pulled up to the front door of Kohl's.

"How's that for service?"

"Terrific. Thanks for listening to me," I replied as I opened the back door of the cab and paid my tab. "Keep the change. I won't make you wait while I shop. I might find you dead when I get back."

Al looked at me with a frown and a disapproving face.

"I'm just kidding. It was a joke."

I stepped into Kohl's and walked to the men's section to find myself a nice dark suit. There was a friendly salesman who kindly helped me.

"What kind of suit are you looking for?" the salesman asked.

"I'm needing a dark suit for a funeral—perhaps a pin-striped one or a solid black."

"I am sorry to hear of your loss."

"Thank you."

"What size do you wear?"

"I wear a size 42 regular with a pants waist size of a 38 and a length of 30 inches."

"Will you need a shirt and tie?"

"Yes, could you please pick out some choices?"

"What size on the shirt?"

"I'm a 16 ½ collar with a 32-inch sleeve."

I stood around the store looking at several suits. It seemed like the longest time before the salesman returned.

"Okay, what do you think about these?" the salesman asked as he held up three suits for me to choose from. He had also chosen a nice selection of shirts and ties.

I stared at all three. I slowly studied each suit and imagined what I would look like in each one. There was a dark black suit with subtle pin stripes, a solid black suit, and then there was the light solid black one.

"I'll take the dark black one with the pin stripes."

"Great. It's your lucky day. The suit won't need any alterations because it is sized perfectly for you."

"That's a good thing because I need it in a few hours for the funeral I'm going to."

"And what shirt and tie do you like?"

My eyes were fixed on each shirt and tie combination as I slowly studied them.

"I'll take the white shirt with the red-striped tie to brighten things a bit."

"Great."

"I do have a special request. Could I pay for the clothes and change in your dressing room since I'm in a hurry to get to the funeral?"

"I don't see why not."

"Wonderful."

The salesman directed me to the checkout counter, where I handed them my merchandise and a credit card. They checked me out, handed me a receipt with my clothes, and I changed into my new suit. I placed my khakis and polo shirt into the bag and headed out the door of Kohl's to call a cab. I checked the clock on my cellphone and it read 12:04 p.m. It looked like I had a little time to grab some lunch.

The cab arrived quickly.

"Where you going?" the driver asked.

A Travesty of Justice

"I'm hungry. Is there a good meat and threes around here, where locals dine?"

"Why, yes, my favorite, Becky's Kitchen."

"What's so great about it?".

"Everything Becky makes is made from scratch. You won't be disappointed."

"Okay, how far is it to paradise?"

"It's about five minutes from here," he replied with a laugh.

"Take me there, please."

"You've got it," the driver said as he sped away to my destination.

It was a silent drive to the restaurant. The driver didn't say a word. He must have been preoccupied with something, or maybe I made him feel uncomfortable.

It didn't take long, and we arrived in front of Becky's Kitchen.

"Thanks, buddy. Here's your money with a tip," I said as I handed him some bills.

I stepped out of the back seat of the cab and walked in through the front door. There was a crowd waiting.

"Man, this is a popular place," I said to the hostess who greeted me.

"You can say that. Folks come from miles away to get a taste of Becky's cooking. Once they get a taste, they're back for more."

"How long a wait?"

"It will be about 15 minutes. But, if I were you, I would definitely wait. It is worth it," she said confidently.

"You've got it."

"Your name, please?"

"Green, Louis Green ma'am."

"You aren't by any chance the Louis Green—the one they call *America's Hero* are you?"

"That's me, ma'am."

"So you're Louis Green, *America's Hero*. Could I have your autograph?"

"Why certainly," I said as she handed me a marker and

asked me to sign a menu.

"Anytime, ma'am," I said as I sprawled my *Louis Green* across the front of the menu.

Time seemed to fly. The next thing I knew they were calling my name to seat me at a table.

"Green, party of one," the hostess said.

I followed her a few feet to a booth.

"The waitress will be here shortly to serve you."

I studied the menu while I was waiting. Everything looked so good.

I was interrupted by a pretty red-haired waitress who was tall and slender. She appeared shy and seemed to be slightly nervous around me.

"I'll be your waitress. My name is Alison. What can I get you to drink?"

"I'll have some water and a cup of coffee black."

While she went to get my drinks, I turned my head slightly to the one o'clock position and noticed a group of waitresses giggling and staring at me. They were pointing directly at me.

My waitress returned with my water and coffee.

"What will you have today for lunch?"

"I'd like the Salisbury Steak."

"What sides would you like with that?"

"I'd like the green beans, mashed potatoes, and corn please."

She stood there for the longest time staring at me as if I was a rock star.

I broke the silence and stare.

"That will be all, thank you," I said as she giggled.

I sipped my coffee and tried to relax, but all I could think of was the funeral service today and what I was going to say for Hershel's tribute.

I was deep in thought and time slipped away. Next thing I knew; the pretty red-haired waitress was bringing me my lunch.

"Here you go, sir. Here's your Salisbury Steak and veggies," she said sweetly.

"Thank you, Alison. I'm Louis Green."

She giggled shyly and replied, "I know who you are. You're

A Travesty of Justice

America's Hero. I've seen you on so many news channels. And I saw you on the *After Hours Show* a few months ago."

"Good memory, and yes, everything you say is true."

"Wow, I can't believe I'm standing here in your presence. You're famous," she said with a soft, sweet, and excited voice.

"Oh, it's really nothing."

"What do you mean that it's nothing? You're a brave man, Louis Green. You freed all of those hostages and saved a lot of lives. I'm nervous to be around you."

"That's mighty kind of you," I said as I took some bites of my lunch. "This food is great! It reminds me a lot of my late wife's home cooking."

Alison kept staring at me. There seemed to be an instant chemistry between us as we continued to talk. She was young enough to be my granddaughter. And here I was striking up a conversation and possibly even flirting with her. She spent a lot of time with me talking. We laughed together, and I'm pretty sure she wasn't on her break. She was supposed to be working, but she was spending time talking with me.

"Alison, I enjoyed talking with you. You are a lovely young lady. I wish I could talk longer, but it's about 1:00 p.m. I have to be at a funeral at 2 p.m."

"A funeral. I'm so sorry, who passed away?"

"He was my brother-in-law, who was the senior pastor at the Church of God here in Omaha."

"I am so sorry, my condolences to you."

"Yeah, it was tragic how it happened. But I am sorry that I need to interrupt our conversation. I need to be at a funeral, and I am fairly sure that I am taking you from your work. It was nice to meet you. Could you give me the check?"

"Sure, I'll be right back."

It wasn't long before she was back at my table. She still appeared shy and nervous.

"Here's the check, Mr. Green."

"Call me Louis."

"Okay, Louis, here's my number in case you want to talk sometime. I'm not usually this bold. I'm rather shy," she said as she handed me the check and a note with her phone number on it.

"I've got to go, Alison. Maybe we'll catch up later."

"I'd like that," she said as she smiled at me.

I left money with a large tip on the table with the check and strutted confidently out of the diner. I had met a new friend today. Sure, she was young enough to be my granddaughter, but she took a lot of interest in me, she was genuine, and very pretty. I was flattered that someone that young could take an interest in me.

I reached for my cellphone and called a cab.

A cab was there in front of the diner in less than five minutes. I opened the door and jumped into the back seat.

"Where are you headed?"

"Take me to the Church of God on North 24th Street."

"Sure, we'll be there in about 15 minutes. Are you going to a wedding?"

"No, a funeral."

"I'm sorry to hear that. Was it a friend or family?"

"It was my brother-in-law who was killed a week ago."

"Was it an accident?"

"No, he was murdered in his own house. Someone set it up to look like a suicide, but it was definitely a murder."

"That's terrible, sir. My sympathies to you."

"Thank you."

"Here we are at the Church of God," he said as he pulled the cab up to the front door. "The place is packed. The parking lot is completely filled. Must have been a popular guy."

"You could say that. Thanks for the lift. Here's the tab and keep the change," I said as I handed him some bills.

I opened the back door of the cab and stepped out. I entered the front door of the church. There stood Cousin Janie and her husband from Atlanta.

"Louis, I am so glad to see you," she said as she gave me a warm embrace.

"Good to see you too, Janie."

"You remember my husband, Ted, don't you?"

A Travesty of Justice

"Yes, I certainly do."

"This is a sad day having to bury Hershel," Janie said.

"I know, I'm still in shock over the whole thing," I replied.

I was greeted by many other family and friends. Some I hadn't seen in years.

"Will Norris and Julie be here today?" Janie asked.

I was taken back and fumbled for the right words to say.

"You must not have heard the news. Norris and Julie have been gone for over six weeks."

"You mean, they disappeared?"

"Yes, they mysteriously disappeared. They never showed for work. I haven't seen them since I ended up in Methodist Hospital in a coma."

"Louis, that's awful. Dear God, what do you think happened to them? People don't just up and disappear."

"I've filed a missing persons report with the Omaha Police Department, and I'm hiring a private investigator to find them."

"Dear God, I'm so worried for them," Janie said.

"Me too," I replied.

"If there is anything I can do to help you, Louis, please let me know."

"I will. So I take it that you hadn't heard from or seen Norris, Julie, or Hershel in a while either."

"No, not since Thanksgiving. And it's so tragic about first losing Aunt Hilda and now having to lose Hershel."

"It's unbelievable," I replied.

"Excuse me for interrupting, but the service is getting ready to start. Please take a seat, so we can close the doors," one of the ushers said to us.

I walked to the front of the church and took a seat where the sign said: RESERVED FOR FAMILY.

The organ prelude music began playing. I stared in disbelief at the closed rosewood coffin lying near the altar.

I still can't believe Hershel is dead.

The organ music stopped and a tall gentleman stepped up to the podium. He was the associate pastor of the church, Pastor Ted Boswell.

"It is a sad occasion for us today to have to bury our brother, Hershel," the pastor said.

Every seat in the church was filled. There were people standing in the back, and people packed tightly in the balcony.

"At the same time, this is a celebration of life for our dear brother, Hershel. He now joins his dear wife, Hilda, in Heaven. Jesus and the angels are welcoming him into the Kingdom of God. You can hear them say the words, 'Well done, my faithful servant.' Let us pray."

Pastor Boswell said some prayers to comfort the family and friends.

Then there was a long pause. I could hear wailing and haunting voices over the silence.

A slender and attractive young woman stood and sang a sweet rendition of the *Lord's Prayer* with the piano. As she sang, my mind wandered back to all the fond memories I had of Hershel and Hilda. I wept profusely and silently. Tears streamed down my face.

Then Pastor Boswell rose to the podium.

"Are there any family members or friends who would like to say a few words in tribute to Pastor Hershel?"

There was a renewed moment of silence.

Then Cousin Janie stepped up to the podium.

"I'm Janie Walker from Atlanta. I'm Hershel's niece. Hershel was a servant to God. He was most generous in helping those in need. There wasn't anyone who didn't love him, and there wasn't anyone he wouldn't go out of his way to help. That was the kind of man he was. I will dearly miss him."

The congregation became completely quiet. The church was still and silent.

Cousin Janie broke down in a flood of tears and wept openly. She couldn't continue her tribute, so she returned to her seat.

I was nervous. My leg and hands were shaking as I rose from my seat. I slowly approached the podium.

"I'm Louis Green. Hershel was my brother-in-law. He was a faithful husband to Hilda. Hershel was an outstanding pastor at

A Travesty of Justice

this church. He was a friend to me. I still can't believe that he is gone. He always treated me with utmost respect. Hershel was one of the most loving human beings I have ever known in my lifetime. I still don't understand how anyone would want to murder someone as decent, respectable, and loving as he was."

All at once I froze. My voice cracked and wavered with deep emotion. I was overcome with what seemed like rivers of tears.

"Hershel, I am sorry for all of the cruel and mean words I said to Hilda during Thanksgiving. I hope you will find it in your heart to forgive me. I love you so much," I said as I held my head down trying to hide the tears covering my face.

I couldn't finish my tribute anymore because I lost it. I left the podium and returned to my seat.

After a brief moment of stillness, a portly, elderly man slowly rose to the podium, trying to keep his balance with his cane as he walked.

"I'm Dean Wellingham. I have known Pastor Hershel for a very long time. He found me one day at the Rescue Mission about 17 years ago. I had lost my family, my job and had no place to go. I was hungry and Pastor Hershel fed me. He and Hilda took me in. They let me stay at their house until I could get back on my feet again. I began attending this church shortly after that. Pastor Hershel led me to Jesus and God. I am grateful. I owe it all to him for saving my life. Pastor Hershel, brother, I love you. You have served God well. I will really miss you. I know that you are safely in the arms of Jesus in Heaven."

Again, the church was completely quiet.

There were many friends who rose to the podium to pay their last respects to Hershel. Hershel was a friend to everyone. He was adored by everybody.

Then Pastor Boswell stood at the podium and prayed.

"Heavenly Father, thank you for our dear beloved brother, Hershel. Please deliver comfort to his friends and family. Please reassure them that he is now safely with your son in Heaven. He has finished his work here on Earth. You have called him to your kingdom with these words, 'Well done, my loving, faithful servant.' We thank you for giving us Pastor Hershel to us even if it was for a short time. We are grateful for having been graced with his presence. May Pastor Hershel rest in peace as we wait for the return of the resurrection when it is time. We say all of these things in your holy name we pray. Amen."

After Pastor Boswell finished praying, he asked everyone to rise as the pallbearers walked to the front of the church and lifted Hershel's coffin to carry it to the hearse that waited outside the church. They carefully heisted it into the back of the hearse. I joined the crowd of family and friends who slowly exited the church. I rode with Cousin Janie and her husband in their car. We followed directly behind the hearse. The hearse pulled out of the church parking lot followed by a line of cars with their headlights on as we made our way to the cemetery. A motorcade of police motorcycles led the funeral procession down North 24th Street toward Westlawn-Hillcrest Cemetery. Onlookers and bystanders who knew Pastor Hershel saluted him as the hearse passed them. Some waved American flags as the hearse went by. It was a moving tribute to Hershel.

We turned onto Center Street Road as the hearse led the way up a hilly narrow road into the cemetery. We parked next to the plot marked by the tombstone where Hilda was buried near a thick area of large trees. Everyone waited until they had lifted Hershel's coffin and placed it by the freshly dug grave beside the tent that was erected for the graveside service. His family and friends all gathered beside the grave. Janie, her husband, and I took a seat on the front row across from the casket. We waited for Pastor Boswell to start the service. Everyone was bundled in their coats as a chilly wind swept through the crowd.

"We are gathered here today to pay our final respects to our dearly beloved brother, Pastor Hershel. It is tragic how he was brutally murdered in his own house and framed to look like he had killed his own self. But unfortunately we live in a dark and evil world," Pastor Boswell said.

As he continued his eulogy, I thought I was seeing things. I caught a glimpse of something moving in between the thicket of trees straight ahead. All at once, there was an angel with wings

A Travesty of Justice

with a sad look on her face as if she were warning me of imminent danger. The hair on the back of my neck stood straight up. A wave of chills ran straight through my body. I recognized that same warning from the angel in my previous encounters. I knew it was a bad sign—a warning sign of danger up ahead. I tried to focus on the words of the pastor, but I was too distracted.

"Hershel was a dedicated, loving and faithful..."

Suddenly Pastor Boswell was interrupted by loud, rapid noises that sounded like gunfire, which could be heard throughout the cemetery. The pastor was struck several times in the chest, head and throat. He was drenched in blood, took his last breath, and collapsed directly over Hershel's coffin, which was next to the grave. The crowd was screaming and crying.

"Someone, help, help. The pastor has been shot. He isn't breathing!" a woman screamed at the top of her voice.

Everyone was running in every direction in a myriad state of panic. The gunfire continued. All at once, two men rushed me. They grabbed Janie, her husband, and me. They hid us behind a clump of thick trees and began returning fire with their automatic weapons. There were bullets flying everywhere.

"Stay down and don't move," one man commanded.

I reached for my phone and called 911.

"Help, the pastor has been shot," I screamed into my cell phone.

"What's your location?" the 911 dispatcher asked.

"We're in the Woodlawn-Hillcrest Cemetery on Central Street."

"Stay calm, don't panic, we are on the way."

"It's a war zone out here. Bullets are flying everywhere!" I shouted at a rapid pace.

Suddenly a bullet hit my cousin Janie in the shoulder. She screamed from the deep agonizing pain.

"She's been hit. We've got to move her now. We can't hold their gunfire much longer," one of the men said as he continued to return fire with his weapon.

"We're outnumbered," the other man said as he continued

to return fire with his automatic weapon.

One of the men who was firing his automatic weapon, helped move Janie, her husband, and me to an elevated area located behind a large stone mausoleum. He never once stopped firing. Once he had us moved, he positioned himself behind the mausoleum so as to avoid being hit by a stray bullet.

"We need backup at the Woodlawn-Hillcrest now. Officers are under attack. One person has been shot," the man radioed ahead.

As the two men continued to return fire with their automatic weapons, I tore off my shirt and made a tourniquet to wrap around Janie's shoulder to stop the bleeding.

It's a wonder we didn't all die that day. There were bullets flying everywhere. The trees and the mausoleum we were hiding behind were riddled with bullets from the attackers. The concrete and the tree bark were all torn to pieces.

We could hear the sirens of police cars as the rescue vehicles headed our way.

And then it happened. It was completely quiet—no more gunfire, no screaming. Everything was calm. Apparently when the assailants heard the sirens, they took off. They knew they might be outnumbered or that they would end up being killed or arrested.

Backup police cars arrived followed by emergency rescue vehicles.

"Is everyone okay? Is anyone hurt?" an officer asked as he rushed toward us.

"The Pastor has been shot. He fell backwards on the coffin!" I shouted.

The EMT paramedics rushed to Pastor Boswell's body to see what they could do to help him.

"My cousin, Janie, has also been shot in the shoulder," I said.

More paramedics rushed to help her and place her on a stretcher. They took her to the ambulance where they whisked her away to the hospital.

It looked like there were 15 police cars, five ambulances and one fire truck that showed.

A Travesty of Justice

There were at least 20 police officers on the scene helping terrified people and searching the area for the assailants.

"There must have been at least 10 of them. But I didn't get a look at them because they were firing continuously with some heavy firepower," said the man who earlier protected us.

"Hi, I'm homicide detective, Pete Sully," he reached out to shake my hand.

"I'm Louis Green and these are my family members."

"You are all lucky to be alive. It is sad and unfortunate, but the pastor didn't make it. He was struck in the chest, and the head. When the last bullet struck his throat he died immediately," Mr. Sully said.

"Those bastards, they'll never get away with this," I said angrily.

Detective Sully paused without saying a word.

"You can all come out from behind the trees and tombstones. You are safe now!" an officer shouted.

Faces peered out from behind the trees and tombstones. There were over 80 people who were miraculously still alive. No one was hurt except for my cousin Janie and Pastor Boswell who was killed instantly.

The police officers helped to comfort those who were victims. Many of those people were in a serious state of shock, and others were sobbing with joy just to be alive.

When they learned of the brutal murder of their pastor, they openly wept and threw themselves on the ground in disbelief.

"That was a disgraceful and savage way to end a funeral of someone you respect and love," I said to the detective.

"You're absolutely right, Mr. Green, it is disgraceful," said Detective Sully. I shook my head in disgust at the tragedy.

"Did anyone here get a description of those attackers who opened fired on you during the service?" he asked.

"I did, sir," a woman stepped forward.

"What is your name?" Detective Sully asked.

"I'm Karen Gilmore. When the shooting started, I ran as fast as I could for the top of the hill in the wooded area above the gravesite."

"You mean up there in that area?" Sully asked as he pointed to high ground surrounded by a woods.

"Yes, I was at a vantage point and saw the whole thing after they shot Pastor Boswell."

"How many were there and what did they look like?"

"It looked like an army of them. There were perhaps 11 or so men dressed in military-style, camouflaged clothing. They came out of nowhere."

"Were they tall, short, dark hair, blonde?"

"They were tall, and large build. I couldn't tell their age or hair color because they had ski masks over their heads."

"Anything else?"

"Yes, they came out of nowhere as if they were hiding in the woods just waiting for the funeral service. They had high-powered automatic weapons, the kind the army uses."

"You mean like rifles?"

"Yes, like M-16 automatic rifles."

"Those are difficult to get but not on the black market."

"They were scary looking. I would call them terrorists."

"They might have been members of some underground group or the mob," Detective Sully said.

There was an immediate pause between Karen Gilmore and the detective.

"They headed back into those woods on the opposite side of the hill."

"Okay, thanks, Ms. Gilmore. I will need your address, phone number and email address so I can contact you later."

"No problem, glad to help."

"Take some canines with you and search the entire wooded area up there for any suspects or evidence," Detective Sully ordered the police officers.

They took a team of 12 police officers armed with M-16's and five dogs up the hill. They began searching through the thickly-wooded area. The dogs were onto a scent of some kind and led the officers through a trail that led out into an open field.

"Which way, now?" an officer asked.

"Let's follow where the dogs lead us to," another officer

replied.

The dogs led the officers through a field the size of football field, and they came to a subdivision on the other side, which was at the end of a cull de sac.

"Look at those tracks they left. Someone burned some rubber getting out of here fast," an officer said.

"Looks like two sets of tracks," another officer replied. "They left in at least two vehicles."

"They could be anywhere by now since the interstate is close by."

"Maybe someone in the neighborhood saw them leave," said another officer.

The officers walked from door to door asking neighbors if they had seen anything suspicious. They finally found a man who identified himself as Marvin Grimley.

"Sir, I'm with the Omaha P.D. Did you see anything suspicious about an hour ago?"

"I sure did. I was going to watch the game on T.V. when I heard this loud squeal of rubber burning on the road. I looked through the blinds to see what all the commotion was about," Mr. Grimley said.

"About what time was that?" he asked.

"It was around 2:40 p.m. I caught a glimpse of a black truck which looked like a Chevrolet Tahoe speeding off through the cull de sac at a lightning speed," Mr. Grimley replied.

"Was there anything unusual about the Tahoe, or did you get a license plate number?"

"No, but there was another vehicle packed with about five men dressed like soldiers with camouflaged clothing and ski masks over their heads. They took off after the first one left."

"Anything unusual about that vehicle?"

"Yes, it was definitely a black Tahoe, and it was jacked up off the ground. It was probably three feet off the ground. It had gold trimming and gold hubcaps."

"Hmm...I see," the officer said as he wrote it all down on his pad.

"Did you get a license plate number?"

"No, it sped away too quickly."

"Thank you for your time, sir."

The officers continued their search and investigation. They had a few leads but nothing solid yet.

Since Cousin Janie and her husband were rushed to the hospital, I had no ride. When I finished talking with the police, I called a cab on my cell phone. It was almost 3 p.m. and I was beat.

Another traumatic day in the life of Louis Green. When will this all end?

The last person had left the cemetery. The police were wrapping up their search and investigation. Here I was alone again.

What an awful, horrible way to end a funeral, particularly for your brother-in-law. Someone's got to pay for this.

But this traumatic episode that happened today wasn't even close to what was in store for me up ahead. My thoughts were interrupted when the cab pulled up in front of me.

CHAPTER TEN

24/7 PROTECTION NEEDED

A loud, continuous knock at my hotel room door woke me up out of a deep sleep. I turned over in bed and without my glasses it appeared that the clock read 9:02 A.M.

Who would be banging on my door at this hour of the morning — and on a Sunday morning?

I rolled out of bed, picked up my glasses from my night stand and peered through the tiny hole in the door. It looked like police officers.

"Who is it?" I shouted.

"It's the Omaha Police, open up."

I cracked the door with the chain hooked. I peered through the crack.

"Show me your badges," I demanded.

The officers placed their badges close to the crack in the door so that I could take a good look at them.

"Okay, you're good," I said as I opened the door wide to greet them.

"I'm Detective Sully. Remember me?"

"How could I forget you. You saved my life."

"Yes, and your cousin's and her husband's."

There was a pause in the conversation.

"Could we come in?"

"Why, yes. The room's a mess, but I'm sure you've seen worse. Sit down."

Three police officers joined Detective Sully and pulled up a chair in my hotel room.

"I guess you're wondering why we're here."

"Yes, I am."

"Remember when you were discharged from Methodist Hospital last week we specifically asked that you accept 24-hour police protection?"

"Yes, I do."

"Do you remember someone at the police department telling you that you were in grave danger?"

"Yes."

"Well, it's been almost a week and you're still running around freely, doing this and that without any protection."

"I didn't think it was necessary after I bought this .45 automatic with extra ammo."

"Well, you thought wrong. Did you see how hard it was for us to keep those attackers from killing everyone at that funeral yesterday? It was almost impossible. We were outnumbered, outgunned, and we had .45 automatics, but that didn't stop them. If it wasn't for the 911 call and the siren sounds blaring loudly, there would have been a massacre."

There was complete silence in my hotel room. I thought about what he had said.

"Do you realize who you are up against, Mr. Green? Do you know who your enemy is? If you don't, I'll remind you."

"You don't have to say more. I get it."

"You should have gotten it a whole lot sooner. Then we wouldn't be in the mess we are in right now. You've got some dangerous, ruthless, scumbag enemies, Mr. Green."

"Yea, I guess I don't need any friends when I've got enemies like that," I quipped.

"Mr. Green, this is a serious matter. We don't need any jokes from you."

"Sorry, sir."

"From here on out, whether you accept it or not, the Omaha Police Department will be providing you with 24/7 protection. We will basically be your bodyguards, like the Secret Service. Wherever you go, we will be there with you. Whatever you do, we will be there protecting you. You can still keep your .45 as added protection, but we are here to make sure you are safe, courtesy of the City of Omaha."

"Okay, let's do it. I accept."

"I'm glad you came around to seeing it our way and that you've finally come to your senses."

"Thank you."

"There will be an officer positioned outside your hotel door. There will be an officer stationed in the lobby as well. Officers will be watching over the hotel and will be parked outside in the parking lot. Some of the officers will be plain clothes men and others will be in uniform. Here is my number. You must call it anytime you are planning to leave the hotel. I need to know when you are coming and going."

"Okay, thank you, sir. I'm sorry that I sounded ungrateful before. But I am truly grateful to you for saving my life and continuing to protect it."

"You're welcome, Mr. Green. We've got some rough times ahead. You're going to be a constant challenge to this police force as we try our best to protect you. Good day, Mr. Green." Detective Sully and the officers left my room and closed the door behind them.

CHAPTER ELEVEN

PROTECTED

I forgot to turn my cell phone off and the ring woke me in my hotel room. I reached for my glasses on my night stand first, but I couldn't get to my phone in time. The clock by my bed read 9:15 a.m. It was already Monday morning. I threw the covers back and rolled out of bed. I tried to focus on the missed call, but I was still yawning. I dialed the number.

"Stan Westerfield, private investigator, how may I help you?" the pleasant female voice said on the other end.

"Someone called me no more than five minutes ago," I replied.

"What's your name?"

"This is Louis Green."

"Why, yes, Mr. Green, we just called you. Mr. Westerfield wanted to set up an appointment with you about your missing son-in-law."

"Oh, yes, I left a message with you. Mr. Westerfield comes highly recommended from the Omaha Police Department."

"If you don't mind me saying so, he is one of the best around. He's located many missing people in his 25 years of detective work. He has an amazing track record for finding missing people still alive and well."

"Well, we'll see how good he is. My son-in-law, his wife and children have been missing for over six weeks. This seems to be a difficult case to solve."

"Mr. Westerfield is always up for a challenge."

"He's definitely got a tough case to crack this time."

"How about meeting at 3:30 p.m. this afternoon?"

A Travesty of Justice

"That should be perfect. Where are you located?"

"Our office is located at 2209 22nd Street North. Mr. Westerfield has requested that you bring anything you can find on your missing family: photos, birth certificates, Social Security cards, bank account numbers, passports, etc. This will definitely help him in his search for your missing family."

"Okay, will do."

"Thank you. We look forward to meeting you."

It was already 9:45 a.m. I hadn't eaten breakfast, and I needed to shower and dress. I had planned on visiting Janie in Methodist Hospital, and now I also needed to stop by Norris and Julie's house to collect any photos and documents I could find.

I jumped into the shower and gave myself a quick wash down. I quickly shaved, washed my face, and brushed my teeth. I put on some khaki pants and a yellow, long-sleeve polo shirt. I almost forgot I had to call Detective Sully. I picked up my cell phone and dialed his number.

"Yes?" he answered.

"Detective Sully, I need to go to Methodist Hospital to check on my Cousin Janie, you know the woman who was shot in the shoulder on Saturday while attending my brother-in-law's funeral. And then I need to stop by my son and daughter-in-law's house to look for photos and documents for the private investigator I have hired."

"Of course, no problem, Mr. Green. There's an officer outside your door. Follow him down to the lobby, and we will take it from there."

"Thanks, Detective Sully."

"Any other requests, Mr. Green?"

"Yes, I need to stop by Stan Westerfield's office. I have a 3:30 appointment today."

"You mean Stan Westerfield, the private detective?"

"Yes, that's the one."

"Ok, you've got it Mr. Green, I will see you in a few."

I opened my hotel room door and was greeted by a big, friendly smile from the officer who was standing outside my door.

"I'll take you down to the lobby," the officer said after he shut my door.

We walked together conversing in small talk as we took the stairs down to the lobby.

"Here we are. These officers will escort you out to the parking lot."

Detective Sully greeted me in the parking lot and helped me into his squad car.

"Okay, Mr. Green, where to first?"

"Take me to Methodist Hospital, please."

Detective Sully turned left onto Main Street and headed to Methodist Hospital.

"Wait a minute. Hold on. I'm hungry. I haven't had breakfast, and I could sure use some coffee."

Detective Sully pulled over into a parking lot.

"Okay, Mr. Green, please make up your mind. Where are we going?"

"Sorry, sir, I haven't eaten breakfast and I'm hungry. Could we please run through McDonald's drive thru?"

"Certainly, Mr. Green."

Detective Sully headed to the first McDonalds. We went to the drive-thru and ordered breakfast and coffee. It hit the spot. I was ready to take on the day now.

"Thank you, Detective."

"You're welcome. Now, where are we headed, to the hospital?"

"Yes, take me to Methodist Hospital, please."

Detective Sully continued driving until he reached the hospital. He parked the car, and we walked to the main entrance. I was accompanied by two other officers as we entered the hospital. Two other police cars parked outside of the hospital watched for any suspicious activities.

After checking with the main desk, we took the elevator to the sixth floor and walked the long hallway until we found room 625. I tapped on the wide, solid-wooden door and opened it slowly.

A Travesty of Justice

"Hi, Janie," I said as she smiled at me.

Her husband, Ted, also flashed a smile at me. He was seated beside her bed.

"Louis, thanks for coming to see me," Janie said.

"I wanted to check on you, Janie. That was terrifying what happened at Hershel's graveside service. We could have lost you."

"You're telling me, Louis. I never thought you cared that much about me."

"Why would you say such a thing? Of course I care about you. You have a strange religion, but I won't hold that against you Janie."

Janie laughed.

"You've always had a way with words, Louis."

"Well thank you Janie."

"How is your shoulder?"

"It hurts like hell, but I'll live."

"So Louis, who's your friend?" Janie asked referring to the police officer who stood beside the door.

"He's my bodyguard."

"Funny, Louis. Seriously, though, who is he?"

"Ever since I was attacked in Los Angeles and then again in the cemetery during the funeral service, the Omaha Police have been providing me with 24/7 protection. They fear that my life is in danger."

"Wow, Louis, I had no idea."

"Now you know."

"Any word on Norris and Julie?"

"No, not a word. That's why I'm hiring a private investigator. I'm meeting with him today. Speaking of which, Janie, I have an appointment in a little while with Mr. Westerfield, so I need to run."

I reached over to hug Janie and gave her a kiss on her forehead. I shook Ted's hand.

"Bye, Janie. I will keep checking on you."

"You better, Louis. Do me a favor, stay safe and out of harm's way."

"I'll do my best."

I walked out of the room with the officer following me as we headed to the elevator. We took the elevator to the lobby on the first floor and several officers followed me out to the squad car.

We got in and then Detective Sully asked, "Where to next, Mr. Green?"

"I need to stop by my son and daughter-in-law's house."

"Where's that?"

"2126 Cedar Point Road, please."

"Okay, we're enroute."

Detective Sully led the way with the other officers' cars following behind. The 15-minute drive went by quickly. Next thing we knew, we were pulling into Norris and Julie's house. Their cars were still parked where they had left them over six weeks ago. The officers followed me up the steps to the front door. They drew their pistols and pointed them toward the door as they slowly opened it.

"Mr. Green, please stay outside with the officers while we check out the house. We're going in first. You never know who could be waiting behind this door."

I stood outside on the front porch with the other officers while Detective Sully and his team searched the house. I stood there for what seemed like a very long time. Then Detective Sully returned.

"It's all clear, Mr. Green. You can follow me."

We stepped into the kitchen. There was a pungent, foul smell that permeated the whole house. There was the decomposed food still sitting in the pans on the stove and in the sink. As we moved to the dining room, we noticed the fully-set table with clumps of flies and gnats hovering over what appeared to be molded food on the plates and mold in the drinks. The setting was eerie.

"Unbelievable. I've never seen anything like it," Detective Sully said as he guided me upstairs into Norris and Julie's bedroom.

"Look, Julie's purse is sitting here on their bed. Her driver's license, credit cards, checkbook and cash are all in there."

A Travesty of Justice

I took those items out of her purse and placed them into a bag Detective Sully had brought.

"These are items Mr. Westerfield requested I bring to today's appointment."

I took the framed family photo that was sitting on their dresser. Then I opened the closet door and opened the file cabinet. I pulled out what appeared to be some birth certificates of each family member. I found some recent photos of my missing grandchildren. I collected everything I could find that might help Mr. Westerfield locate my missing family.

"I think I got enough for Mr. Westerfield," I finally said.

"Looks like you do, Mr. Green," replied Detective Sully.

"I'm ready to go Detective."

"Okay, let's hit the road." He led the way outside and closed the stained-glass front door behind us. As he did, a large German Shepard dog climbed the front steps and approached us. There was something strange about the dog. A large, bulging, brown paper bag was attached to the plain unmarked collar of the dog.

"Where the hell did this dog come from?"

"I don't know; I've never seen him before."

The detective reached down and carefully untied the bag from the dog's collar.

"Good boy, nice dog. Stay," the detective said as he tried not to anger the dog or get bitten.

The dog was restless and tried to run, but Detective Sully was able to remove the bag.

"Bet you a hundred dollars, there are dog snacks in here," Detective Sully.

Without warning, silence swept in as Detective Sully's eyes and face froze with shock as he opened the brown paper bag.

"What the hell, a real severed hand with a golden wedding band on it."

All I could do was stare in sheer terror.

"Is this some kind of sick joke?" I asked.

"Apparently so."

"Let me see that ring on the finger."

I studied the ring carefully. There was something familiar and unusual about the ring. It was riveted with a familiar pattern unlike any other man's wedding band. Also, the hair and shape of the arm was familiar.

All at once, I fell apart as I recognized the golden band. I couldn't contain myself as fear, anger, rage, terror and helplessness overwhelmed me.

That ring was Norris's wedding ring, which means it had to be the severed hand of my son.

His hand was sent as a sign or warning. Was Norris still alive or had he become a victim of some sick, psychopathic killer? And were Julie and my grandchildren still alive? Sooner or later I would learn the truth.

CHAPTER TWELVE

THE PRIVATE INVESITIGATION BEGINS

My day was totally ruined after witnessing Norris's severed hand delivered to me in a brown paper bag by a strange stray dog in the neighborhood. Detective Sully took photos of the hand for evidence.

"I'm sorry that this hand could be the hand of your son," Detective Sully said.

"Me, too. This is chilling, bone chilling," I replied.

"Whoever has your son and family are some dangerous professionals. They are a powerful force to be reckoned with."

"That is what scares me the most."

"No matter how angry you might be right now; it is important not to jump to conclusions."

"Why shouldn't I? It's my son's hand!"

"There is a possibility that it might be his hand and then again it could be someone else's. We won't know for sure until we run a DNA test on it."

"I know my son's hand when I see it."

"Okay, but even if it is your son's hand, it is possible that he could still be alive."

At that point I became very quiet. I wasn't sure how to respond.

"We need to get you to your appointment with Stan Westerfield," Detective Sully said as he looked at his watch.

He helped me into his squad car and closed the door. He started the engine and headed out to the highway.

"We'll get there in time for your 3:30 p.m. appointment."

I still remained silent and refused to talk with the detective.

We drove a while until we reached Main Street. The other police cars followed.

"Here we are, Mr. Green," the detective said as he pulled into the parking lot where the sign read: STAN WESTERFIELD, PRIVATE INVESTIGATIVE SERVICES.

We stepped out of the squad car and closed the doors behind us. I was surrounded by the "bodyguard" policemen as we walked up the front steps that led to the large Victorian-style house to reach the offices of the private investigative services. As I entered the large, beveled-glass, mahogany door I was greeted by a slender, attractive blonde woman who wore black-rim glasses. She sat behind a large, ornate, mahogany desk as she greeted me with a smile.

"I'm Louis Green, and I'm here to see Mr. Westerfield. I have a 3:30 p.m. appointment."

She stood and reached her hand over the desk to shake my hand.

"I'm Lori Westerfield. Welcome to our private investigative services. Please take a seat, and Mr. Westerfield will see you shortly."

I took a seat in the lobby, and the other officers sat around me. Several officers remained outside watching the building carefully for any suspicious activity.

"Are you kin to Mr. Westerfield?" I asked.

"Yes, I'm his oldest daughter. This is a family-run business, and my dad likes to keep it that way."

"I see."

I waited patiently and quietly.

"Mr. Green, Mr. Westerfield will see you now."

"Thank you."

A tall, muscular and sturdy-looking man with dark hair and glasses greeted me with a firm handshake. He resembled Clark Kent of Superman.

"I'm Stan Westerfield. You must be Louis Green."

"I am Louis Green."

"Follow me back to my office."

Detective Sully and several officers followed me to Mr.

A Travesty of Justice

Westerfield's office, and we took a seat.

"Wow, Mr. Green, you have quite a following with all of these bodyguards," Mr. Westerfield said.

"I can't help it. It must be my natural attraction," I quipped.

"Well, whatever it is, I can see that they are taking this matter seriously."

There was a lull in the conversation. During the silence, I took a moment and studied Mr. Westerfield's office. There were plaques, degrees, and awards covering his walls. There were piles of files and paperwork stacked on the floor and on his desk. I could tell he wouldn't win an award for neatness.

"So did you bring the documents and photos that I asked for?" Mr. Westerfield asked.

"I sure did. Here is a whole bag full of stuff."

I handed him the bag, and he sorted through it looking for documents and photos that interested him.

"How recent is this photo?" Mr. Westerfield asked as he held up a family portrait.

"That was taken about five months ago."

"How about these photos?"

He held up individual five by seven photos of my grandchildren and separate photos of Norris and Julie.

"Those were all taken about the same time—five months ago."

"Good-looking family, I must say."

"Thank you. God, I miss them."

"I'm sure you do. How long has it been since you last saw them in person?"

"I saw all of them on Thanksgiving Day and through the middle of the next week. So many awful, God-forsaken events happened during that time."

"Like what?"

"We were all gathered together around the table on Thanksgiving Day to celebrate a feast. Suddenly my sister Hilda was choking on something she ate. She turned blue in the face and then passed out. We worked frantically to give her medical help. We called 911, and they rushed her to the hospital. We spent 14 hours waiting on news about her. Then we left to return to my son and daughter-in-law's house only to find it completely ransacked. It was trashed beyond anything you could imagine with obscenities written on the walls, flooded rooms and the despicable act of decapitating our pet cat."

"Unbelievable," Mr. Westerfield said.

"Oh, there's more," I said.

"More?"

"On Monday I went to cash my Social Security check and ended up almost losing my life being held hostage by five masked men."

"How did you break free?"

"There was this angel who helped me."

"An angel. Surely, you don't believe in angels, Mr. Green?"

"Now I do."

"Wow, well that's some story."

"Then I started getting calls from news stations, and late-night talk shows. I was in demand for being credited for saving all those people in the bank."

"Are you telling me you didn't save those people?"

"Again, no, it was an angel who intervened."

"I've heard everything now, Mr. Green. Angels don't exist."

"Sir, no disrespect, but angels are as real as I am sitting here looking at you."

"Well, you're entitled to your opinion."

"Thank you. Then on Tuesday, I spoke at my sister's funeral. She didn't survive the choking episode at our Thanksgiving Day celebration dinner."

"I'm sorry."

"I am, too, because Hilda was a wonderful sister. We didn't always agree on a lot of things, but she was a great person. I didn't treat her right."

"How so?"

"I always made hurtful remarks about her weight."

"Was she obese?"

"Oh, yes. She had a severe weight problem. She weighed at least 350 pounds to put it politely."

A Travesty of Justice

"Oh, I see."

"The last time I saw my family in person was that following Wednesday, almost a week from Thanksgiving. I kissed them and told them goodbye. I left in my truck for Griswold, Iowa. There I was greeted with a hometown hero's parade. As I was speaking to the crowd in the Griswold Community Center, the mayor was shot in the arm. It turns out that bullet was meant for me. I was supposed to die that day."

"So, an assassin was after you?"

"Yes, I just didn't know it at the time."

"I learned later from television news reports and from the police that the killer was a dangerous, psychopathic fugitive who had escaped from the Nebraska State Penitentiary."

"Why do you think he was trying to kill you?"

"The Los Angeles Police and the Omaha Police are still trying to determine that reason."

"Why the Los Angeles Police?"

"It's a long story, but I was invited to be a guest on the *After Hours Show* and suddenly I was getting all kinds of offers to appear on different shows. I realized it wasn't safe to be traveling everywhere, and I didn't have the time nor energy to do it all. I concluded that if I had to choose one show to make a guest appearance it was going to be my all-time favorite show, the *After Hours Show*."

"Fascinating."

"After the Griswold Police discovered the identity of the psychopathic fugitive killer and that the killer wanted me dead, the Griswold and State Police provided me with 24/7 protection."

"What is the fugitive's name?"

"T. Bone Jones. He has outsmarted the FBI, the police, and detectives for quite some time."

"Tell me more about your Los Angeles visit."

"Oh, yes, on my flight to Los Angeles I discovered that the killer was on the same plane."

"How did you know for sure?"

"There was this angel who suddenly warned me about

him."

"An angel, yeah right. I told you there are no such things as angels."

"Believe what you want to believe, but I saw an angel in the back of the plane standing in front of the restroom."

Mr. Westerfield let out a roar of laughter. He couldn't contain himself about my angel story.

"Believe what you want to believe, Mr. Westerfield, but there are definitely angels out there. One day, I promise you, you will discover this truth."

"Well, let's put it this way, I've never seen one nor have met anyone up until now who has seen one. They don't exist."

"Back to the story on the plane, I hid in the restroom and locked the door until the angel told me it was safe to open the door."

"Okay, go on," Mr. Westerfield said with a foolish grin on his face.

"The angel warned me that the fugitive killer was sitting several rows behind me. She said that he had disguised himself so that no one would recognize his face which was shown all over every television news network."

"What happened next?"

"The flight attendants thought I was a terrorist. So the captain radioed to the tower in Los Angeles. The next thing you know, when we landed, I was apprehended by Homeland Security and every police officer in Los Angeles."

"You're lucky you didn't get locked up."

"I was escorted off the plane by a squad of armed officers. I was taken to the Homeland Security/TSA Office in LAX and questioned for a long time. When they learned that I was a guest on the *After Hours Show*, they changed their tune."

"How so?"

"They treated me better. They said they had recognized me from all of the television news networks as *America's Hero*."

"You suddenly got the royal treatment?"

"Yes, they were suddenly nice to me. They let me go, and it's a wonder I got to NBC in time for the show. I was running very

A Travesty of Justice

late. Luckily, I was the last guest on the show."

"So what happened to the fugitive killer?"

"As I was getting ready to appear on the show, I was about to turn my cell phone off. I got this text from someone who said they were in the audience and would kill me after the show. I was petrified but went on the show anyway."

"Wow, some story."

"Yeah, and in the middle of the interview, I appeared rather foolish on national television. As I looked out into the audience I saw what appeared to be an angel with a bright light in the back of the auditorium. It seemed to be a warning to me.

I blurted out that someone in the audience was trying to kill me. It was an embarrassing moment for everyone. The camera people and producer tried to cut me off. They went to a quick commercial break and wrapped up my interview, but the damage had been done."

"That's because when you start talking about angels, most people think you're nuts," Mr. Westerfield said.

"Do you think I'm nuts?"

There was a long pause where neither one of us said a word.

"Well, what happened after the show? Did anyone try to kill you?"

"I asked security to escort me out to the street. I received another text that said the killer was waiting for me. I called a cab, but as the cab door opened, the security guard was rushed by someone who appeared out of nowhere. The security officer was shot in the face, and I took off running. I ran several blocks through dark alleys trying to escape. But it was too much for me. I was tired and out of breath. I jumped up on a hanging fire escape ladder next to a building but couldn't quite get my grip. There I was dangling from the ladder."

"What happened next?"

"The killer had me cornered. He told me that I was going to die. He shot me several times and I fell into a pool of my own blood. He left me for dead."

"Well, you're alive to tell this story. So how did you miraculously survive?"

"Next thing you know I was lying in a hospital bed in Methodist Hospital in Omaha. It was the strangest thing."

"How did you get from Los Angeles to Omaha without knowing it?"

"Apparently, they tell me that I was in a coma for 28 days due to severe brain injuries. They found my body in a pool of blood in the back alley. I was life-flighted to Cedars-Sinai Medical Center in Los Angeles. I spent some time there in ICU, and then I was flown to Omaha where I woke up from a coma in Methodist Hospital. I was surrounded by the staff, and I started telling them the story of what happened."

"Wow, that is some story. It would make a great book."

"Ever since I woke up from my coma, I've been trying to find out how much of my story really happened and how much of it is a dream."

"I've been doing some digging and found out that your brother-in-law was found dead in his house not too long ago."

"Yes, it was very tragic. It happened about three weeks ago. The police found his body upstairs in his bedroom slumped over against the wall in a pool of his own blood. They found a pistol lying next to his body. They discovered a bag of cocaine in his room. There was speculation that the whole thing was suicide, but I know better. I've known Hershel a long time. That's not something Hershel would do."

"Wasn't he a pastor of a large church here?"

"Yes, he was Senior Pastor of the Church of God here in Omaha."

"So, did the police find the true cause of his death?"

"Yes, they finally ruled it as a homicide. They found tracks of mud that led from the outside through the kitchen and up the stairs to his room. They were tracks of a rather large and tall person."

"Do they have any leads?"

"I don't know. They are on the case, and I am supposed to be meeting with the Omaha Police soon."

"Do you think there are any connections with what happened to you, with your missing family, and the homicide

A Travesty of Justice

of Hershel?"

"I don't know. There could be. It appears someone wants me dead and is trying to send me warnings."

"Has anything happened lately?"

"You could say so. About a week ago I went to buy a gun at Guns Unlimited. On our way to the store, our taxi was followed by a black Chevy Tahoe with three men in the vehicle. My taxi driver waited outside the store while I was making the purchase. When I returned to the taxi, I thought my driver had fallen asleep with the taxi running. I tapped on the window to wake him up and discovered that he had been shot in the head several times. He had been executed."

"God, that's awful. It definitely sounds like a warning."

"Yes, and when I was attending Hershel's graveside service last week, his service was suddenly interrupted by gunfire. We were ready to lower Hershel's coffin into the grave when a small army of men rushed the crowd and opened fire. They hit the pastor, who was ending the service with a prayer. His body fell over the coffin. I grabbed my cousin and her husband. We ran for cover behind some large tombstones. Luckily, some undercover police were in the cemetery at the time and returned fire against the attackers. When the attackers heard the approaching police sirens, they escaped toward the woods."

"Did you get a good look at them?"

"They were tall, muscular men. They had ski masks over their heads and wore military-styled camouflage outfits."

"Doesn't sound like they were scared of anything."

"No, in fact on my way over here, we stopped at my son and daughter-in-law's house to pick up some documents for you. When we had gathered everything, we closed the front door behind us. Out of nowhere, a large German Shepherd dog ran up to us. There was a large bulging brown paper bag attached to his collar. We were curious to see what was in the bag. We were horrified when we opened it. We discovered a man's severed hand with a wedding ring attached to its finger."

"Wow, that's the work of organized crime or a terrorist

group," Mr. Westerfield said in surprise.

"When I looked closely I saw that the ring was made of a unique, unusual design. I recognized the ring as my son's wedding band. It was Norris's dismembered hand."

"How horrible that must have been."

"Yes, it was. But the detective said I must not jump to conclusions that it was my son's hand. He is running DNA tests on the hand to see if it matches my son's DNA."

"He's right, it could be anybody's hand."

"I still can't get that picture out of my mind."

"I'm sorry Mr. Green about all that has happened to you."

"Thank you."

"What else did you bring me?"

"I have all of my family's Social Security cards, birth certificates, my daughter-in-laws' credit cards and drivers' licenses, and bank statements."

"This will be useful in my search for them."

"What do you think happened to my family? Any theories or ideas? Surely, you must have some idea."

"The strongest theory is that they were abducted. They could have been kidnapped."

"If they were kidnapped why hasn't anyone stepped forward and demanded a ransom?"

"Maybe they're waiting for the opportune time. They could have been abducted and killed. They could have joined the Church of Scientology and are being held captives, or they could be part of the Witness Protection Program and were suddenly whisked away by the Government. What do you think happened to them, Mr. Green?"

"I think they were..."

Before I could finish my sentence, a loud piercing bullet shattered the window in front of us, smashed a clay vase of flowers into pieces, and struck the wall about one inch from Mr. Westerfield's face. When we realized what had happened, we fell to the floor seeking cover.

"Are you hit?" Detective Sully asked as he drew his gun.

A Travesty of Justice

"No," Mr. Westerfield said.

"Everyone stay down low. There could be more where that came from," an officer said.

The other officers in the building drew their weapons and were ready to return fire.

"It could be a sniper at a distance, too," Detective Sully said as he radioed for backup.

CHAPTER THIRTEEN

THE COMFORT OF A WOMAN

My visit with Mr. Westerfield ended rather badly. There I was in his office trying to get to the bottom of my family's disappearance when we were almost killed by a sniper's bullet. It just proved to me how dangerous my life had become. No matter how many police officers were surrounding me 24/7, it wasn't going to stop someone who wanted me dead.

After the almost-deadly sniper attack, Detective Sully and the police officers escorted me safely back to my hotel. They knew the dangerous force they were up against, and they weren't about to take any chances. I wasn't sure if Mr. Westerfield still wanted to represent me as my private detective after he was nearly killed by a bullet that came within one inch of his skull.

It was almost 7:30 p.m., and I should have been exhausted after the day's traumatic events, but I was wired. There I sat alone in my hotel room with nothing to do. I could have chosen to sit here all night and worry about what could happen to me, or I could do something to change that. I had made a mess of my life. My life was sad and complicated. My hotel was completely surrounded by police officers, and my room had become a prison. I had no freedom. I was a slave in my own world.

I was bored and restless. I reached into my pocket and sifted through my receipts and paraphernalia. I noticed a handwritten note to me on the back of a receipt. It was Alison's phone number. Alison was the young, pretty red-haired waitress who fawned over me in the restaurant I had visited for lunch several days ago.

I picked up my cell phone. I dialed her number. It rang for four times. Then I heard a sweet, affectionate voice on the other end.

"Hello?"

"Is this Alison?"

"Yes, it is. Who is this?"

"This is Louis, Louis Green. I'm the guy you waited on in Becky's Kitchen a few days ago."

"Oh, I remember you," she said as she giggled.

"Well, how have you been?"

"I've been working a lot lately. I need a break."

"Would you like to get together and get some dinner or coffee?"

"Sure. I'd love that."

"How about tonight?"

"Sure."

"There's only one problem."

"What's that?"

"I'm in my hotel room at the Days Inn, and I'm completely surrounded by the police. I'm being protected 24/7."

"Is that because you're famous?"

"No, there's someone trying to kill me?"

"Oh, I see," she replied hesitantly.

"We can still get together tonight. But, I must warn you, it is dangerous to be around me," I said trying to laugh it off.

"That's alright with me. I love danger," she replied flirtingly. "Do you want me to stop by your hotel?"

"Even if you stopped by my hotel, they might not let us out of their sight. Chances are we wouldn't have any privacy, and we probably wouldn't be able to go to dinner."

"Well, what do you want to do, Louis? It's your call."

"I've got an idea. What if you distracted the officers in front of my door? I could disguise myself and slip out the fire door exit without being noticed. Then we could leave in your car. Your car could be parked close by in another parking lot. Are you up for an adventure?"

"Sure, Louis, I love adventures."

"Okay, so here's the plan. Be here at my hotel at 8:30 p.m. Does that give you enough time to get ready?"

"Certainly. I'm only about 10 minutes away from the Days Inn."

We discussed in detail our getaway, escape plan. Then I told her that I would see her later, and I quickly headed for the shower. I washed, shaved, and put on some nice clothes. I brushed my teeth and my hair. I was looking pretty handsome for an old man.

Time zoomed by as I anticipated seeing Alison again. My watch read 8:30 p.m. A text suddenly flashed on my phone screen: "In hallway with officers."

There Alison stood outside my hotel door in the hallway distracting two officers. Alison wore a red mini skirt with high heels, and she had let her long red hair down. Her lilac perfume was inviting. She was laughing and flirting with the officers. At that point, they would have done anything she asked. Her charm, beauty, and words were so enticing that she lured the officers away from my hotel door and was heavily flirting with them in the elevator as they were headed down to the first floor lobby.

Another text flashed: "hallway clear." That was my cue to exit my hotel room.

I put on sunglasses and a long-haired blonde wig that I had found at the Goodwill store in Omaha and knew it would come in handy someday. I looked like a washed-up, old rock star. I opened my hotel room door slowly and peered down the hallway in both directions. There was no one in sight. I shut the door quietly behind me and placed a DO NOT DISTURB sign on the handle of the door. I quickly moved to the fire exit door and sprinted five flights down to the first floor exit door. I opened the exit door slowly and looked in both directions. There were no police guarding the side exit of the hotel. I ran across the back parking lot and down several parking lots until I found my final destination: Cracker Barrel Restaurant. A light-blue Nissan Altima was parked in the very back lot. Headlights

A Travesty of Justice

suddenly flashed as a signal from Alison to meet her. I opened the front passenger door and hopped in.

"It's about time you got here," she laughed flirtingly.

"I had to be careful. I didn't want to get caught."

"You look like Mick Jagger with your wig and sunglasses," she laughed.

I laughed along with her. I was having the time of my life.

"Where to my darling?" she asked.

"Start driving and I'll let you know. We need to go to a place where we won't be discovered."

"I wonder how long it will be before they discover you're missing."

"I hope never."

Alison stepped on the gas, and we sped away to a destination unknown.

"Are you hungry?" she asked.

"I'm starving."

"What are you hungry for?" she asked in a flirting manner.

I paused for a moment. I wasn't sure how to answer her.

"I could go for anything?" I answered.

"Anything?"

"Yes, anything," I replied firmly.

"We're going to have a fun time," she said as she hit the gas pedal doing almost 80 mph up the Interstate.

"Slow down, Alison. We don't want to call attention to ourselves by getting a ticket," I demanded.

"Yes, Daddy," she replied with a seductive giggle in her voice.

We drove for almost an hour on the Interstate but the time passed quickly. We were laughing, joking and flirting with each other.

Finally, we slowed down and took the exit which read, "Lincoln".

"I'm taking you to a special place. Do you like Sushi?" she asked.

"I like anything you like," I replied with a giddy smile on my face.

"Let's do it," she said with youthful enthusiasm.

We drove a little further off the exit and pulled into a parking lot with a bright orange sign that read Fushun Japanese Grill.

"Have you been here before?" I asked.

"Yes, and it is a great place—that is if you like sushi."

"I do."

We parked the car and headed straight for the restaurant. Alison placed her armed entwined in mine. I stopped and opened the door for her with my chivalrous ways.

The hostess seated us at a small table in the corner. It was cozy, dimly lit and there were fresh flowers sitting in a vase on the table.

"How's this?" Alison asked.

"It's perfect."

"Well, here we are," she said with an enthusiastic voice.

"Wow, we're an hour from Omaha, and it's just you and me. No hotel prison walls, no one following me around 24/7, and no police protection."

"We're living kind of dangerously."

Alison couldn't keep her eyes off of me. I could tell that she wanted me, and even if I wasn't exactly sure why, I hadn't felt this excited in a long time, so I played into her desire.

"You're kind of cute with your shades, wig, and rock-star look," she teased.

Before I could reply, the waiter introduced himself and asked what we were having to drink.

"Louis, let's get a bottle of wine," she said.

"Okay, you choose," I replied.

"We'd like a bottle of the Verget Chablis."

"You've got it," the waiter replied.

Then there was silence. Alison's eyes were focused solely on me. I was feeling a bit uncomfortable, but still I loved the attention she was showing me.

"So what were you saying, Alison, something about my shades and wig?"

"I think you're adorable with your shades and wig."

"Wow, I haven't had anyone tell me that in a long, long time."

"Not to mention that you make me laugh, Louis, and I'm having a fun time with you."

"So am I, Alison,"

The waiter returned to our table with a bottle of wine and poured us each a glass.

"Here's to us," Alison said as she raised her glass toward mine.

"Yes, cheers to us," I replied and took a sip of the dry, white wine. "So where are you from?" I asked her.

"I was born in a tiny town called Washington. Last I checked there were only 150 people living there."

"What state?"

"It's in the very southern part of Nebraska, only a few miles from Kansas," she replied.

"Wow, so you're a country girl."

"You could say that. Tell me about you, Louis."

"I'm from Griswold, Iowa. It's a small town of about 1000 people, a bit larger than Washington."

"You seem kind of lonely. What's that all about?"

"I lost my wife Samantha to a long battle with cancer about five years ago. I've been a loner since then."

"I'm sorry to hear that, Louis," she replied in a tender, empathetic way.

"What about you? Have you had anyone you've loved that much?"

"Yes, I have Louis. It tore me up and wrecked my life for three years."

"I'm sorry."

"Don't be. He was a total jerk. He tried his best to control me. I was young and foolish at the age of 18. I should have known better than to fall for his ways."

"How old are you now?"

"I'm 24."

There was a long pause as my brain processed her young age.

"Is there something wrong, Louis?"

At that moment, the waiter returned to take our order. We had been so lost in our conversation and chemistry that we hadn't decided what we were going to order. The waiter told us that he'd return in five minutes.

Alison stared affectionately at me with her inviting eyes. I broke the silence.

"What are we doing?" I asked.

"I don't know, you tell me, Louis. You called me," she replied.

"What we're doing or about to do is scandalous."

"Scandalous, how so?"

"You're only 24 years old for God's sake."

"Yea, so what, we're having fun, aren't we?"

"But, I'm old enough to be your father, maybe even your grandfather."

"You worry too much, Louis, just enjoy the ride. Aren't you having fun?"

"Yes I am. I'm having more fun than I've had in a very long time."

"Well there you go. You answered it," she replied.

"You're absolutely gorgeous Alison. That's what scares me. Why would someone as young, smart, and unbelievably beautiful as you are want to spend time with me?"

"Why wouldn't I, Louis? Don't sell yourself short. You are funny, smart, and good-looking in your own way."

I paused in silence. I thought about what she said about me.

"That's kind of you Alison. But, really, why do you want to spend time with me?"

"I can't explain it, Louis, I just enjoy being with you. Doesn't that count for something? Age is just a silly number."

"I'm afraid I might like you more than I want to admit."

"Well, Louis, I like you too. Let's just have fun. Don't be afraid, it's not like I'm going to marry you or anything like that."

I laughed at her comment about marriage. It broke the tension.

The waiter returned and took our orders.

"Have some more wine, Louis," she said as she poured another glass.

We laughed and relished in the intense chemistry connecting us.

Alison wanted to know everything there was to tell about me. So I obliged and told her. She also shared her stories. I was captivated by every one of her words and body language. We were so entranced in each other that we forgot to eat. It was a very magical moment in my life. I hadn't felt so mesmerized since I had first met my wife, Samantha. After Samantha went to be with Jesus, I gave up on life and on love. There was a giant hole in my heart that had been crying out to be filled with love. And suddenly Alison came into my life. I felt like I had known her from the day I was born.

"Do you want to get out of here?" Alison asked.

I called the waiter over to our table.

"Check, please," I said.

Alison kept staring at me with her inviting blue eyes. As I waited for the waiter to bring me the check, I felt her foot rubbing against my leg under the table. I felt nervous. I hadn't been with a woman in years. I didn't know what she expected from me. I wanted to be her friend. I enjoyed her company, but I wasn't ready for anything more. I paid the check and walked Alison through the restaurant door to her car outside in the parking lot.

Once we were seated in her car, we sat there in the parking lot. Everything was quiet. It was awkward for me. She broke the silence.

"What do you want to do now, Louis?"

"It's kind of late, Alison."

"It's only 12:30 a.m."

"That's late for me."

"Are you tired?" she asked.

"Actually, no, I'm not tired. I'm full of life."

"Well, we could get a hotel room."

"A room for you and me?" I asked nervously.

"Yes, Louis, for you and me. We are grown-ups," she replied.

"I mean; how would that look? An old man checking into a hotel with a young woman?"

"Who cares, no one's watching. Why do we care what people think? It's your life isn't it?"

"You're right, Alison," I replied hesitantly.

"It's too late to drive back to your hotel tonight, anyway. We can spend the night here in Lincoln and get up early, drive back, and sneak you back in to your hotel room before they know you're missing," she suggested.

"Wow, Alison, but we'd only have four hours of sleep," I replied.

"Who said anything about sleeping," she replied with a teasing voice.

I became still and quiet. I gulped a large chunk of saliva down my esophagus out of nervousness and fear of not knowing what would happen next. There was suddenly a rush of adrenaline. I felt like I was 20 years old again.

Alison started the car. We drove around in search of a hotel.

"How about this one?" she asked.

"A Hilton?"

"Why not?" she said as she laughed seductively.

"You're some classy, country girl," I blurted out.

"You could say that."

We pulled into the parking lot of the Hilton Garden Inn located on R Street in the Haymarket area of downtown Lincoln. The hotel was brightly lit and looked very suave for two country people.

"Are you ready?" Alison asked flirtingly.

"Yes, absolutely," I replied.

We walked together hand-in-hand like two love birds who had been together their entire lives. We entered the plush foyer through the grand front door and stepped up to the front hotel desk.

"May I help you?" the front desk attendant asked.

"Yes, we need a room for two please," I replied.

A Travesty of Justice

"Queen, king or double?"

"We need a king, please," I replied.

"Here, fill this card out. I'll need to see both drivers' licenses."

I wrote down all the requested information and handed him our drivers' licenses with a credit card.

"How long will you be staying with us?" he asked.

"Until morning," I answered.

He looked at Alison and then took a look at me at least twice as if he were sizing up the situation that we were about to get into. I can only imagine the pictures that were running through his mind.

"Okay, that will be $245 with tax. You are in room 515. Here's your hotel key cards."

"Thanks," I said.

Alison and I walked hand-in-hand to the elevator and pushed the up button. As we waited, she leaned forward toward my face and gave me a soft and warm kiss on my lips. All at once, I lost my cool. I was like a silly boy back in grade school flirting with the cutest girl in school.

"Did you like that?" she asked as she winked at me.

I couldn't keep from blushing. Giddiness was showing all over my face.

"What do you think?" I replied.

The elevator door opened and we headed up to the fifth floor.

The door opened on the fifth floor and she stopped me again. She reached over toward my face and gave me another kiss.

"If you keep this up we'll never…." I said as I tried to finish my sentence.

"We'll never what?" she asked.

"We'll never get any sleep," I replied.

She suddenly laughed as if what I had just said was amusing. She grabbed my hand and playfully led me down the hallway to room 515.

"Here we are. Step into my office," she said playfully as she beckoned me with her finger.

We opened the door and turned on the lights.

"Wow, look at this room. This is perfect," she said as she playfully leaped onto the bed looking at me seductively.

The curtains and drapes were open wide.

"Look at that view outside. You can see the city lights," I said.

"If you're going to look out the window all night, then I'm going to put my clothes back on," she said as she stood completely naked on the bed.

I turned around and when I caught a look at her shapely, buxom naked body, I covered my eyes.

"We shouldn't be doing this," I said.

"Doing what?" she asked.

"We should take this slowly and get to know each other as friends first," I said.

"Well, don't you like what you see?" she asked as she jumped playfully on the bed.

"Of course I do, but I really want to get to know you first as a friend. That takes some time."

"I am your friend, Louis," she replied as she threw a pillow at me as I stood in front of her petrified.

"Sure you are my friend, Alison, but I don't know much about you. I want to learn everything about you. Can't we just hold each other in bed and talk without doing anything?" I asked.

"Sure, if that's what you want."

"I'd like that," I replied.

"How about I put my bra and panties on and you can hold me," she said in a flirting manner.

"Sure," I said reluctantly.

"Take your clothes off. You can keep your shorts on," she insisted.

I hesitantly removed my shirt, pants, and socks and placed them neatly over the chair. I kept my shorts on. She slowly and seductively slipped her black-lacy, bikini panties up her legs to her thighs as if she were doing a burlesque show. She placed her black-lacy, push-up bra over her firm breasts. Alison stepped off of the bed, walked toward me, and turned around with her back facing me.

"Could you fasten my bra?" she asked.

I slowly walked close to her and fumbled around with my hands trying to fasten her bra.

"If you want me to keep my bra on, you're going to have to do a better job of fastening it."

"There, I got it," I said as I was finally able to snap the fasteners together.

She smiled, kissed me on the lips, and turned off the lights. She gently took my hand and walked me to bed. We adjusted our pillows in the comfortable positions that we liked. She pulled the covers over us and moved close to me. She wrapped her arms tightly around my torso. I could feel her shapely body pressed against my back. It was an amazing feeling to be held again.

"How do you like this?"

"It's perfect, feels wonderful," I answered.

"Louis, I'm crazy about you. Did you know that?" she said as she whispered softly to me.

"Thanks, I feel the same way about you, Alison."

"We can take this as fast or as slow as you'd like. I just know that we're going to be great friends and who knows perhaps others things too," she said.

"Thanks for humoring me. I don't want to ruin the good thing that we've got going."

"You're not going to, Louis. I'm your friend. You can trust me. You can tell me anything. I'll keep it a secret."

"That's awesome, Alison."

We didn't get any sleep throughout the night and morning. She just held me tightly and wouldn't let go. I was loving every minute of it. I opened up and told her all that was going on with me after I awoke from my coma in Methodist Hospital. I told her everything there was to know about Hershel's death, the attack at Hershel's funeral, the investigation of my attempted murder, the disappearance of my son and daughter-in-law, and about finding the severed hand of my son. She listened attentively and took it all in.

The bright sunlight penetrated the room as morning arrived. Alison gently massaged my back and playfully tickled me until I woke up laughing.

"It's time," she said with a gentle voice.

"It's morning already?"

"Yes, and we've got to get you back to your hotel before they find you missing."

"Could we savor this moment just for a few minutes?"

Her gorgeous blue eyes were fixated on mine. Our lips succumbed to gravity, and we slowly kissed passionately until I had to break away.

"What's wrong?" she asked.

"I'm feeling things I shouldn't be feeling at this age."

"Like what?"

"Like feelings I haven't felt in years."

She pressed the front of her body so close to mine that I thought we were glued together.

"Are you referring to what I'm feeling from you right now? Is that what you're talking about?" she whispered seductively.

"Yes, that's exactly what I'm talking about."

"Don't be embarrassed. It's natural."

Alison started kissing me again and pushing against me.

"Okay, that's enough for me," I said as I pulled away and tried to catch my breath.

"You don't have any heart problems do you?"

"No, my heart's perfectly fine. It's just that I want to take it slowly and get to know each other first."

"Okay, Louis, that's fine with me," she said as she stepped out of bed and walked to the restroom.

I could hear the toilet flush, and then I heard the water rushing from the shower.

A few minutes later she walked into the room where I was lying in bed. She was completely naked. Alison dried herself off with a large towel right there in full view for my eyes to see. I must admit I didn't close or cover my eyes this time. Call me a dirty senior citizen or some other name, but I was really into it. She reached for her black-lacy panties and slipped them on. She placed her bra over her breasts and again asked me to fasten her bra. I obliged. She slipped on her red mini skirt and began brushing her hair—all in front of me.

"Okay, Louis, it's your turn to shower and get dressed," she reminded me.

While I was in the shower getting washed up, I was unaware that Alison had been snooping through my wallet and checking out my cell phone. She had time to look through my phone numbers and text messages. As I dried off and put my shorts on, I walked into the bedroom where she was. I noticed that she had quickly put my phone down as if she had been caught doing something she wasn't supposed to do.

"Are you looking for something?" I asked.

"I was just checking out your phone," she replied sheepishly.

"For what? It's just a phone, nothing special."

"I hadn't seen a phone like this is in a while," she said as she tried to make light of being caught.

"Why don't you ask me if you're going to use my phone," I said.

"No worries, Louis. I won't touch your phone again."

"Thank you," I replied tersely, trying not to be annoyed.

She moved in close and gave me a sweet, gentle kiss.

"All is forgiven, it's no big deal," I reassured.

"Okay, good, then we need to get back to your hotel soon. Here's your pants and shirt."

"We can get some breakfast on the way at McDonalds," I said as I put on my shirt and pants.

I quickly brushed my hair and teeth. I reached for Alison's hand and led her out the hotel door. We walked down the hallway to the elevator and took it to the first floor lobby. Alison held my hand as we walked like two silly school kids toward her car. She unlocked the car as we stepped into it. Alison started her Altima and sped away toward the Interstate.

"We should be back in Omaha by 7 a.m.," she said.

We laughed and talked away the hour trip to Omaha.

"Here's the exit to your hotel," she said as she turned off the Interstate.

"Ok, so what's the plan for sneaking me back into my hotel room?"

"I'm going to pull the fire alarm and get them to clear the building," she said as she giggled.

"Don't you think that's risky?"

"Life is a risk, Louis. I'm going to slip into the hotel when everyone is cleared out and let you in through the side fire exit door."

Alison drove her car to the Cracker Barrel parking lot where we met before.

We stepped out of the car and she walked up close to me. She pressed her shapely body against me tightly and gave me a long kiss with her arms around me.

"This is for today, tonight, and in-between the time I see you again," she said.

She reached under her red mini skirt and pulled her black bikini panties down to her feet. She stepped out of them right there in the daylight in the parking lot. She handed them to me.

"Here, this is a gift for you, so you won't forget me."

"There's no way I could ever forget you, Alison."

I stuffed her lacy panties into my pants pocket, and we walked our separate ways toward the hotel.

"Check your text messages. You will know when I open the side fire exit door," she said.

Alison walked through the front door of the Days Inn and walked the hallway of the first floor. I looked over my shoulders and everywhere to make sure the police officers weren't watching me. I waited patiently next to the side fire exit door, again wearing my long, blonde, rock-star wig and sunglasses.

A text message flashed on my phone that read: "Done".

There was a loud piercing sound that blasted the entire hotel. People were rushing in a state of panic out of their hotel rooms to find the nearest exit. Alison sprinted to the first floor

A Travesty of Justice

fire exit door hoping not to be noticed as there were people running everywhere. She opened the exit door, and I immediately ran up the stairs to the fifth floor. Alison ran out of the fire exit door and headed straight to her car.

When I entered the fifth floor, I slowly opened the inside fire exit door to see if the police were there. Apparently, the police had left the hallway outside my room to investigate the commotion. I rushed to my hotel room door and unlocked it with my key card. I closed the door behind me, sat in a relaxed position, and turned on the television.

The loud piercing fire alarm kept blasting throughout the hotel. Next thing I knew, I heard sirens of fire trucks, police, and paramedics arriving to the hotel. There was a loud persistent knock on my door.

"Mr. Green are you in there?" a loud deep male voice shouted.

I took a few minutes to answer the door.

"Mr. Green the hotel could be on fire. You must leave immediately," the voice continued.

I opened the door and several police officers escorted me down the hallway to the fire stairwell. We walked the stairs to the first floor exit and stood outside in the parking lot.

"Mr. Green, you got out just in time," Detective Sully said. He was totally unaware that I had escaped and spent the night in a different hotel in a different city. I couldn't believe that I had gotten away with what I did last night and didn't get caught. I was one lucky guy.

CHAPTER FOURTEEN

RUINED

A loud continuous knock at my hotel room door woke me. I turned over in my bed and stared at the alarm clock next to me on the night stand. Wow, it was almost 10 a.m. I guess my body was telling me I needed the sleep. The loud knock continued.

"Mr. Green, are you awake?" The voice shouted.

I rolled over out of my bed and opened the door slowly. My sleepy eyes peered through the crack in the door.

"What do you want?" I asked.

"I've got some urgent news I need to tell you," Detective Sully said.

"Can it wait?"

"No, it's very urgent. Can I come in?"

"Okay, then," I replied as I unlatched the chain on the door. "Come on in."

Detective Sully and another officer stepped into my room. He had a newspaper in his hands.

"Pull up a chair Mr. Green, we've got some talking to do," he said.

I turned one of the desk chairs around and sat facing the detective.

"Have you seen today's headlines?" Detective Sully asked.

"No, I've been busy."

"Here, read it for yourself," he said as he handed me a copy of the *Omaha World-Herald*.

The headlines read:

A Travesty of Justice

WESTERFIELD INDICTED ON CHILD PORNOGRAPHY CHARGES.

"Why are you showing me this?" I asked.

"I don't know if you are clearly thinking this morning, Mr. Green, but this front-page story is about Stan Westerfield, your private investigator, the one who is investigating your missing family."

"So they got Stan Westerfield?" I asked.

"Yes, the one that is so upstanding in the community."

"How is that possible? Stan Westerfield seemed like a moral and decent family man, not to mention one of the best private investigators this side of the Mississippi," I said with disbelief.

"He's been squeaky clean his entire career," Detective Sully said.

"This is unbelievable," I replied.

"The article claims that his office was raided the day after your appointment with him."

"That's exactly a day after the sniper fired through his window and almost killed him and us both," I remembered.

"Yes, it talks about that, too, in the story. But it also says that the FBI raided his office and took his computer hard drives. They suspected him of dealing in child pornography."

"Unbelievable. You think you know someone but don't really know them at all," I said. "Do you think he did it?"

"No, absolutely not," Sully replied.

"And why is that?"

"Because I've known Stan Westerfield for over 20 years. He is a deeply committed family man who would never in his lifetime get involved in child pornography."

"Well, then what do you think is going on?"

"It's obvious to me that he's being framed. It's all got to be a setup. Someone or some organization has planted pornography on his computer to get him out of the picture, because he is close to finding your missing family and bringing this crime to justice."

"You might be right."

"I know I'm right. Mr. Green, this is no coincidence. Neither is the sniper attack on Mr. Westerfield's office two days ago. The cemetery attack during Pastor Hershel's funeral service and the dead taxi driver who was shot at point blank while you went to purchase your .45 in front of Guns Unlimited are all connected. I believe that they are linked to the Russian mob, Bravta."

"Seriously?"

"Most definitely. At the moment, I can't prove that Bravta was responsible. But my gut instinct tells me something is very wrong here."

"This is getting pretty scary."

"You should be scared, very scared, Mr. Louis. If it turns out Bravta is behind all of this, you are in grave danger. I'm thinking we need to get the FBI in on this. You're going to need more protection then you've got now. If we were smart, we'd put you in the Government Witness Protection Program."

"You really think I should be in the Government Witness Protection Program?"

"Yes. You are a sitting target, Mr. Green."

"This is unbelievable. Now I need to find another private investigator. I need to find my family."

"You do, but I'm not sure who would represent you knowing that they could be in grave danger. Word gets out fast."

"Well what do you think I should do now?"

"Wait a minute, I think I know just the right person to be your private investigator."

"Who might that be?"

"He used to be a gangster himself. Then he changed his ways, and with a plea bargain he ended up working for the FBI. They don't make them any tougher than that man. He is ruthless. Nothing scares him. In fact, he's not scared to die for the cause. He'll go after those son of a bitches tirelessly."

"Do you think he'd represent me?"

"I'll ask."

CHAPTER FIFTEEN

CONNECT THE DOTS

"Glad you could join us today, Mr. Green," Captain Willis of the Omaha Police Department said.

I looked around the conference room and noticed that every VIP decision maker of the police force seemed to be seated at the long wooden conference table. It was very impressive.

"Sure," I said as I took a seat.

"Do you know why you are here Mr. Green?"

"I guess it's about everything that's been going on in my life lately."

"You are correct in your assumption. I have invited Detective Sully, Detective Calhoun and the entire homicide investigative staff of the Omaha P.D. to be here today," the captain continued.

I took another good look around the table and noticed a few people I didn't recognize. Some were standing in the back of the room.

"Oh, and a few higher ups from the FBI will be joining us."

"Good to know," I said.

"Here's what we know so far," Captain Willis said as he directed his eyes toward the large screen in the conference room. He pushed a remote control button to start the slide show.

"This is T. Bone Jones. He is a fugitive still on the run. He escaped the Nebraska State Penitentiary in December. He is extremely dangerous and has been convicted of brutal murders in the past. He was sentenced to life in prison at the penitentiary. He attempted murder several times against Mr.

Green and the Griswold, Iowa, Mayor. T. Bone left Mr. Green for dead in his own pool of blood in Burbank, California, in late December."

"Do you think T. Bone is responsible for my brother-in-law, Hershel's death?" I interrupted.

"We'll get to that in a moment." Captain Willis advanced his presentation to the next slide. "This is Alexander Cherkesov. He used to work for the KGB until they were dissolved. He found organized crime to be very profitable, and he is a mastermind in money laundering and racketeering. Cherkesov is what we call an international operator, meaning that he circulates between Russia, Germany, Asia, and the United States."

"So what does he have to do with anything?" I asked.

"Mr. Green, if you'll be patient, I'll explain everything about my theory in a moment. We're trying to connect the dots right now." He took a deep breath and continued to the next slide.

"This is Sergei Ivanov, a brutal, deadly killer. He is an ace marksman sniper. Ivanov could hit a flea moving on someone's shoulder at a mile away. That is how incredibly good he is. He is responsible for countless assassinations by sniper gunfire. He has operated all over the world in terrorist-related crimes. Right now he is believed to be operating in the United States."

"In this next slide is Boris Dubkova. He towers over 6 feet 5 inches in height. He is a mastermind drug smuggler. He deals in cocaine, hash, heroin, and ecstasy primarily. You name it, and he can get it for you. He has connections all over the world. He deals in volume shipping through cargo ships that arrive in ports worldwide. Notice the large deep scars on his face. He double-crossed another mob member and they carved his face out like a jack-o-lantern."

Captain Willis continued his slide show proudly gracing us with the mug shots of another four mobsters whom he was investigating in his "connect the dots" theory.

"And finally this is who we've all been waiting for. Pictured is the feared evil leader of Bravta, master of all crimes, Viktor Levkova. He is believed to be currently somewhere in the United States. There is a five-million-dollar bounty on his head.

A Travesty of Justice

Every underground organization from here to Beijing wants him dead or alive."

Then the slide show came to an end, and someone turned the lights on in the room.

"What do all of these men have in common when you connect the dots? They are all top echelons of the Russian mob, Bravta," Captain Willis said.

"That's good to know. But what does that have to do with all that has been going on in my life?" I piped up.

"Good question, Mr. Green. We believe that when you stopped the five masked men that day in the Bank of Omaha heist-hostage takeover back in December, you interrupted a master plan they had in place for over a year."

"What are you talking about?" I asked curiously.

"You see, those five masked men worked for Bravta. They weren't in that bank to only rob it. They had other plans much bigger than staging a robbery," he continued.

"Well, like what kind of plans?"

"Have you ever heard of suitcase bombs, Mr. Green?"

"I don't think I have. What are they?"

"They are Russian nuclear devices. They are portable nuclear bombs," Captain Willis explained.

"Excuse me, but did you say nuclear?"

"I did indeed. They have an explosive charge of one kiloton. One kiloton is equivalent to 1,000 tons of dynamite."

"Did you say 1,000 tons of dynamite?"

"Yes, 1,000 tons of TNT is enough explosive material to destroy everything in a half mile radius. That means all of downtown Omaha would have been wiped off the map. Every building you see standing here today would be nothing but a pile of rubbish."

"That is frightening," I said.

"You better believe it is. And the horrifying part is that if a good wind picked up the nuclear fallout, it could have carried the radiation miles from the affected area. It wasn't a coincidence that the masked men chose that Monday in December to rob the Bank of Omaha. The weather reports indicated that there would be high winds of up to 55 miles per hour. Had they been able to detonate that bomb, they might have been able to contaminate a whole area from Omaha to Denver, Colorado; from Omaha to Oklahoma City, Oklahoma; and from Omaha to as far away as Chicago, Illinois. We are talking about over 20 million people being contaminated with nuclear radiation," Captain Willis said.

"Hell, you're talking about a major catastrophe," Detective Sully interjected.

"How did you know they were planning to blow up the bank with a suitcase bomb? I didn't see them carrying any briefcases or other items other than their high-powered weapons," I said.

"After they were captured, we found the nuclear suitcase bomb in what was supposed to be their getaway car," Detective Calhoun said.

"They didn't bring the suitcase bomb into the bank at first because they didn't want to be conspicuous," Detective Sully theorized.

"We believe the plan was for one of the masked men to run out to the getaway vehicle, grab the suitcase bomb, and bring it back into the bank to place it perhaps by the teller windows. And Mr. Green, you had to go and bust the whole thing. They didn't get a chance to carry out their terrorist plan. So I would say that the name they call you *America's Hero* fits you perfectly," Captain Willis explained.

"I would say they were furious and still haven't gotten over it," Detective Sully said.

"They sent T. Bones Jones out through a jail break to kill you because you not only interrupted their master plan, but you made them look like fools," Captain Willis continued.

"T. Bone almost succeeded in killing you, but you are a strong-willed man, Mr. Louis. You hung in there for 28 days while you were in a coma, and you're alive today to tell your story. You make the perfect witness in a trial. That's why you're number one on their hit list," an FBI agent interjected.

"One of the Bratva hit men got your brother-in-law and

A Travesty of Justice

made it look like it was suicide. It could have very well been T. Bone Jones, but I suspect the giant, Boris Dubkova. The trail of mud footprints left in Hershel's house were a size 14 boot. That is a large fellow," Detective Calhoun said.

"This is all such a tragedy," I shuddered.

"If I had to use my educated guess, I would say Hershel's murder was an act of revenge against you and your family for T. Bone Jones not being able to put you six feet under," he continued.

"The dangerous killers of Bravta have been either wiretapping you or have had spies watching you because they seem to know all of your moves," Captain Willis said.

"How so?" I asked.

"Look what happened when you rode in that taxi to Guns Unlimited. There were three men in dark suits in a black Tahoe following you. Most likely they were Bravta. You go into the store to buy the gun and come out to the taxi to find your driver shot in the back of the head, execution style," Captain Willis explained.

"And look what happened at your son's house when we went there to collect all of those documents. A German Shepherd approached us carrying what we believed to be your son's severed hand in a wrapped brown paper bag. That was another warning sign from Bravta for you to back off of your investigations, Mr. Green. Turns out the DNA reports show that the hand we found was not your son's hand, which makes it even more mysterious. Now we are dealing with possibly another homicide," Detective Sully said.

"What do you think happened to Norris, Julie, and their kids?" I asked.

"I think they were abducted by Bravta. They either have been brutally murdered and are buried deep beneath the ocean floor, or they are still alive and being held hostage for ransom which they will be demanding later," Captain Willis said.

"Have you noticed that they haven't killed you yet, Mr. Green? They have attempted to send you many warnings but haven't been successful in knocking you off," Detective

Calhoun said.

"The vicious attack in the cemetery during Hershel's graveside service and the sniper-attempted assassination attack the other day are all marks of Bravta," Detective Sully said.

I froze in disbelief.

"Hell, even the trumped-up charges of child pornography against Stan Westerfield are most likely the works of Bratva," Detective Sully continued.

"They are ruthless, cold-blooded scumbags," Captain Willis interjected.

"Yea, that Westerfield indictment is nothing more than character assassination at its finest," Detective Sully said.

"So when you connect all of the dots, you get one mother of an evil, terrorist organization called Bravta," Captain Willis emphasized.

"This is terrifying," I trembled.

"You said it, Mr. Green. We know who committed all of these heinous acts of crime, but we're not exactly sure how to stop them or indict them. It's nothing but a travesty of justice," Captain Willis said as he shook his head.

"Meanwhile, we've got to find an effective way to protect you, Mr. Green. "Would you be willing to participate in the Government Witness Protection Program?"

CHAPTER SIXTEEN

FIREBALL IN THE SKY

The next day I was awakened by a loud voice frantically shouting from behind my door.

"Mr. Green, wake up, wake up," the voice continued to shout as someone pounded on my hotel room door.

I turned over in my bed, reached for my glasses, and noticed that the alarm clock on my night stand read 6:02 A.M.

I reluctantly rolled out of bed and slowly opened the door to see who was pounding on my door.

"Turn on the T.V.," Detective Sully demanded.

I grabbed the remote and turned on the T.V.

"We have breaking news from this upscale Omaha neighborhood," the reporter said. The news flashed to a live camera shot of a house totally engulfed in flames.

"We are coming to you live from Cedar Point Road, where a witness reported seeing a fireball-like explosion light up the twilight sky this morning about 5:32 a.m.," the reporter continued.

"I was up early jogging when this massive fireball erupted," the man said as he spoke to the reporter live on camera.

"Where did you first see the explosion?" the reporter asked.

"It came from those houses," the man said as he pointed to the house that was still towering with tall, visible flames.

"Almost every firefighter in Omaha is here trying to battle the flames which have spread to a few of the neighboring houses," the reporter said.

"Get dressed quickly, Mr. Green. We are headed to Cedar Point Road," Detective Sully demanded.

I threw on yesterday's clothes and didn't bother to brush my hair or teeth. We were in a big hurry and all that could wait.

I followed Detective Sully and several police officers down the hallway, to the elevator, and out the front door of the hotel. They escorted me into their police vehicle, and we sped away to Cedar Point Road. We were followed by a whole entourage of police cars.

We arrived on the scene to a crowded block of people standing in their pajamas, gawkers, reporters, and camera crews.

"Which house was hit first?" Detective Sully asked a bystander who was dressed in his pajamas.

"That one," he said as he pointed to the house overcome with flames.

"What's the address?" Detective Sully asked.

"2126 Cedar Point Road."

"Mr. Green, isn't that the address of your son and daughter-in-law's house?" the detective asked.

I stared at what was left of the frame of a house totally engulfed and raging in flames.

"Oh my God, it's unrecognizable. How could this happen?" I asked in disbelief.

I broke down in a flood of tears. Emotions overcame me like I hadn't experienced since I lost my dear wife Samantha. I fell to my knees on the sidewalk by the curb. I couldn't take it anymore. I felt defeated. This was Norris and Julie's beautiful home. There were precious treasured memories that built this house. It was the only home my grandchildren knew. Now it was all gone, along with my son, daughter-in-law, and family. I continued to weep in disbelief.

"I am sorry for your loss, Mr. Green. I know it must be difficult for you right now," Detective Sully said.

For a while, I couldn't say anything. Then I shouted.

"Damn those bastards of Bravta. I hope every one of them rots in hell," I angrily shouted raising my arm and clenching my fist.

"I can only imagine the anger and hurt you feel," the

detective replied.

"You're damn right, I'm angry and hurt. Those lowlife scumbags have done nothing but torment me and ruin my life."

"Mr. Green, I assure you that their day in hell is coming. We've just got to get them first before they get us," the detective said.

"I hope they burn in hell."

"Mr. Green, right now they're giving each other high fives. They think they've beat us. But one day here soon we're going to get the last laugh when we take them down," the detective tried to reassure me.

"Come on, Mr. Green, let's go to the police station. We've got some planning to do. We're meeting at 10 a.m. to strategize our next plan of action," he said as he led me to his unmarked police car.

CHAPTER SEVENTEEN

CONTIGENCY PLANS

"It's 10 a.m. and it looks like we are all present for our contingency plans meeting today," Captain Willis said as he looked around the long wooden table in the Omaha Police Station conference room.

The room was packed with all of the VIP detectives and high-ranking officers. Several key FBI agents were present as well.

"We're got a problem, one big, gigantic mess. It's called Bravta. They are wreaking intense havoc on our city with attacks and murders, not to mention all of the trafficking that's going on with drugs, money laundering and racketeering," Captain Willis began.

"The FBI and the Omaha P.D. are working on a plan to eradicate Bravta and all of their mob leaders. But, first we need to get Mr. Green relocated quickly through the Government Witness Protection Program. Our current 24/7 protection plan through the Omaha Police is not working," the captain continued.

"We've got a plan in place for you, Mr. Green. How soon can you be ready to start?" an FBI agent asked.

"I can start today if you'd like. What do I have to do to get ready?"

"You'll need all of your belongings packed by Friday. We're going to change your looks and your identity," the agent said.

"Have you ever thought of becoming a woman?" Captain Willis asked with a grin.

A Travesty of Justice

I paused for a few seconds and considered what he had said.

"I can't say the thought ever crossed my mind," I replied.

"Well, you're going to have to keep an open mind when you enter the Witness Protection Program. You'll be living a whole new life with a whole new identity," Captain Willis said.

"I guess I'll try to keep an open mind."

"Do you know what Bravta could do to you, Mr. Green, if they captured you alive?" the FBI agent asked.

"Something terrible, I know."

"They would probably dismember your body and run it through a commercial-grade meat grinder. We're not talking about some low-level mob here," the FBI agent emphasized.

I paused for a minute. The thought of my body being dismembered and run through a meat grinder sent shock waves through my entire body.

"Alright then, make me into anyone that you want to make me into," I said.

"You've got it Mr. Green," the FBI agent said.

"We plan to change your name to Jessica Tompkins. How do you like that name?" Captain Willis asked.

"Well, I never thought of being a Jessica. But it sure beats going through the meat grinder."

"We plan to fit your face with a deluxe, full-form silicone skin mask," the captain said.

"Seriously?"

"Oh, yes, and we are designing a full-length, brunette wig that looks life-like. Did you ever see the film *Mrs. Doublfire*?"

"Can't say that I have."

"Well when we finish with your new identity, we're going to top *Mrs. Doubtfire*. No one on this planet will ever recognize you," Captain Willis said.

"Here's the best part. We're moving you to Duckwater, Nevada, population 334," the FBI agent said.

"But there's nothing to do there," I replied.

"Precisely."

"What will I do while I'm there?"

"Absolutely nothing. You're going to lay low until we fry these low-life, scumbags," the FBI agent said.

"How long is that going to take?"

"It could take a long time. So get used to a nothing-of-a-town kind of life, Mr. Green. It sure beats being all ground up like ground beef."

"We're working on your new ID and other document changes now," Captain Willis said.

"And then I will be the new me, Jessica Tompkins," I said sarcastically.

"You won't have any contact to the outside world—no cell phones, no computers, no landline phones, no contact period," Captain Willis said.

"Seriously?"

"Yes, seriously. That's how our Witness Protection Program is managed. We'll have a whole new wardrobe for you to choose from—dresses, skirts, blouses, and pant suits."

"I'll stick with the pant suits," I said reluctantly.

"Anything else we need to cover?" Captain Willis asked.

"Yes, how will you or the FBI contact me to know if and when the evil culprits have been apprehended?"

"Don't you worry about that, Mr. Green. When the government wants to find you, they will find you. You know the old saying, 'Don't call us, we'll call you,'" he replied.

"Oh, there is one very important subject that we missed entirely, Mr. Green," Captain Willis said.

"Tell me, I don't want to miss anything."

"We're going to have to kill you off, and kill you soon," Captain Willis said with a grin.

"Excuse me, did you say you were going to have to kill me. Whose side are you on anyway?"

"Mr. Green, we were referring to your staged death," Captain Willis explained.

"Staged death?"

"Yes, we are going to stage your death before we move you to Duckwater, Nevada. It's going to be well-publicized so that Bratva honestly believes without a doubt that you're really dead."

I paused and sat there thinking about what he just said.

"Don't worry, you won't feel a thing. You're going to die in a high-speed car accident on Edward Babe Gomez Avenue, and it's going to happen soon," the FBI agent interrupted.

CHAPTER EIGHTEEN

"YOUR SECRET'S SAFE WITH ME"

I was startled by a loud knock at my hotel room door. I was trying to catch up on the news with the T.V. blaring and wasn't paying attention to what was going on around me.

"Room service, Mr. Green," the voice spoke loudly from behind the door.

The clock on the wall read 11:52 a.m.

I grabbed the T.V. remote and lowered the volume. I put the remote down and walked to the door. I opened it slowly and peered through the space between the attached door chair and the adjoining wall. The maître d' was standing in the hallway holding a large covered silver tray close to his shoulder.

"Lunch is served just for you, Mr. Green, compliments of the hotel," he said with a smile.

"It's safe to eat, Mr. Green. I checked it out. I took a small bite of everything. I can tell you it is mighty good," Detective Sully said.

I opened the door for the maître d'. He carried the tray and set it on the table next to the desk. I handed him a ten-dollar bill for his generosity.

"Thanks, sir. Please let the hotel know that I appreciate this very much," I said.

"Thank you, sir, have a wonderful day," he said as he closed the door behind him.

I sat at the table in anticipation of what I was about to eat. I placed a large napkin on my lap and lifted the cover to discover an extra-large Philly Cheesesteak sandwich on a long hoagie bun. It smelled delicious. There was a large helping of fries and

A Travesty of Justice

coleslaw next to the sandwich. And the hotel threw in a large slice of pecan pie with whipped cream on top.

Wow, that is so nice of the hotel.

I picked up the sandwich and took a bite. It tasted amazingly great. As I chewed it, I felt something stiff pressing against the roof of my mouth. It was coarse. I immediately spit it into my hand. As I sifted through the food in my hand I discovered a torn piece of paper. I lifted the bun off the sandwich. Lying between the onions and peppers was a folded note neatly tucked under the meat. I pulled the note out and unfolded it.

Handwritten in cursive with black ink, it read:

DO YOU LIKE MY BLACK PANTIES? DO YOU MISS ME? I MISS YOU! MEET ME OUTSIDE THE HOTEL AT 8 P.M. SHARP—SAME PLACE BY MY CAR. DRESS LIKE YOU DID BEFORE. THE HALLWAY WILL BE CLEAR AT 8. TAKE THE FIRST FLOOR FIRE EXIT. I WANT YOU!

It was signed with the initial A. All at once a picture of beautiful, sexy, red-haired Alison appeared before me in my mind. All of the amazing memories of the last time I spent that exquisite night with her in that Lincoln hotel came back to me. I went to my dresser and opened the top drawer. I sorted through the small pile of socks and boxers. I found her black-lacy panties. I picked them up and held them close to my face. They felt soft. Her lavender perfume still lingered on them. I was in deep thought.

I couldn't wait to see Alison again. She stirred up every feeling that I hadn't felt in years. Her sensuality made me feel like I was 25 years old again. I wanted her badly. Yet, it felt wrong. Alison was young enough to be my oldest granddaughter. That was shameful for a man old enough to know better. I was torn as to what to do. A part of me said, "No, leave her alone, she's trouble." The other part of me was greatly attracted to her adventurous spirit, her youthful beauty, and her sensuality. I was drawn to her, and I couldn't help myself.

I was tired, so I decided to take a short nap. I dreamt about sweet Alison.

A loud voice from the T.V. shook me out my dreams. Apparently I had leaned back against the remote, which was wedged between the back of the chair and my back. I had accidentally turned on the T.V. I woke up to reality. The clock by my bed read 7:35 p.m. I had been asleep and lost in my dreams with Alison for hours. If I was going to meet her at 8 p.m., I needed to get ready.

I threw my clothes off and jumped into the shower. I washed and dried myself. I brushed my hair and teeth. I placed the long blonde wig over my short hair and put on my favorite blue jeans. Then I dressed into my favorite tropical silk shirt. I left my shirt tail out to look more like a rock star. I placed my sunglasses over my ears and nose. I looked at myself in the mirror. I was one cool-looking dude. I was ready to party. The clock on my cell phone said it was 7:59. The anticipation of seeing Alison again was staggering.

As soon as the clock read 8:00 p.m. I opened my hotel door slowly and peered in both directions through the space in the door. The hall was clear as Alison had said. I quietly closed the door behind me and placed the DO NOT DISTURB sign on the outside handle. I sprinted down the firewall stairway to the first floor. I slowly opened the side fire exit door to see if any officers were around. There was no one in sight. I closed the outside fire door and made a dash for the Cracker Barrel parking lot which was located three parking lots down from the hotel. I spotted Alison's blue Altima. She flashed her headlights from the back parking lot. I couldn't contain myself. I opened the front passenger side door and hopped in. My face was flushed with a giddy look. I couldn't hide my desire for her. Alison leaned over with a seductive smile on her face. She wrapped her arms around me tightly and gave me a long, wet, deep French kiss. I surrendered.

Finally, after that exuberating kiss, she released her arms and started the car engine.

"Did you like that?" she asked.

"You bet I did."

"There's more where that came from," she said with a seductive voice.

Before we pulled out of the parking, Alison reached under her red mini skirt and pulled her red-thong panties down to her legs. She stepped out of her thong with her left foot and then lifted her right foot off of the gas pedal. She stepped completely out her thong. Then she twirled her thong around on her right hand index finger seductively.

"I won't need this tonight," she said as she handed her panties to me.

I just about lost it. She was hot and wanted me. I was speechless. I tucked her red thong into my pants pocket.

"We better get out of here before they discover that you're missing," she said as she realized I wasn't buying what she was trying to sell.

Alison stepped on the gas as we sped out of the parking lot and onto Interstate 80 headed west.

"Where are we going?"

"It's a surprise. You'll love it."

"I can't wait."

"So, Louis, what have you been up to lately?"

"My life's a terrible mess. I'm trying to get myself out of all this trouble."

"Why don't you tell me about it?"

"It's top secret. I can't even tell my own mother."

Alison moved her body closer to mine. She reached over with her hand and starting rubbing my neck with her fingertips. The sensation was overwhelming. I could feel every hair on my skin stand straight up. I was drowning in ecstasy. I was lost in our own little paradise.

"Could you at least give me a hint?"

"I'm afraid not."

Alison ran her hands down my back and rubbed it with her fingertips. She pressed her lips up against my left ear and whispered into it.

"If you tell me, I'll make love to you all night long," she moaned seductively.

I felt torn between keeping my word to the FBI and my desire to tell her so I could sleep with her. I wasn't thinking with my brain anymore. I was intoxicated from Alison's seductive ways. I wanted her so badly that I couldn't take it anymore. So I did the unthinkable. I went against my better judgement. I betrayed the FBI, the Omaha P.D., and my own self.

"Okay, I'll tell you. Have you ever heard of the group Bravta?"

"Can't say I have."

"They are a powerful Russian mob. They have networks all over the world. There are over 300,000 of them worldwide. They are involved in money laundering, racketeering, prostitution, and illegal drug distributions."

"Wow, so tell me more," she prodded.

"They are the group that's responsible for all the awful stuff that has been happening to me," I confessed.

"What kind of stuff?"

"It all started with a crazy psychopathic killer named T. Bone Jones. He broke out of the Nebraska State Penitentiary and tried to kill me."

"Why was he trying to kill you?"

"Bravta put me on their hit list as revenge for breaking up their Bank of Omaha robbery-turned hostage crime back in December," I explained.

"I remember that well. The title they gave you, 'America's Hero' is so accurate. You are definitely a hero in my eyes, Louis" she said proudly.

"That's kind of you, Alison. It turns out the motive was not to rob the bank. The bank heist was only a front for their greater plan. When the five masked men entered the bank, they were supposed to make it look like a bank robbery. They never planned on me ruining their plans and getting them apprehended."

"What kind of ulterior motive did they have in mind?"

"While the masked men were robbing the bank, one was supposed to leave the bank and return with a suitcase bomb,

A Travesty of Justice

which the FBI found later in their getaway car. But I prevented the masked gunman from planting that bomb in the bank."

"What's a suitcase bomb?"

"A suitcase bomb was invented by the Russians, and it's very powerful. It has explosive power equivalent to 1,000 tons of TNT. There have been reports by the news media that nuclear suitcase bombs are merely fiction and don't exist. But, believe me, this one was real. It contained enough plutonium to do maximum damage," I explained.

"Wow, so they were planning on blowing up the bank, huh?"

"They chose that Monday in December to carry out their attack because all the weather reports predicted high gusts of wind up to 50 MPH. They knew they could do the maximum amount of damage and devastation with that kind of wind."

"How so?"

"You see, a suitcase bomb when detonated releases deadly nuclear radiation for miles. If the wind had blown as strong as they had predicted for that Monday in December, it could have contaminated cities as far away as Denver and Chicago. But it turns out the weather reports were wrong."

"Wow, that's scary. We're talking about millions of people being affected," she said.

"Try 20 million people," I replied.

"That many, huh?"

"20 million. Now you can see why Bravta is a little upset at me," I said with a chuckle.

"It's kind of obvious."

"That's Russian terrorism at its finest," I said sarcastically.

There was a lull in our conversation as Alison continued to rub my back with her finger tips. She started humming a pretty little tune.

"Not to change the subject, but how did you manage to clear the fifth floor hotel hallway at exactly 8 p.m. tonight?" I asked.

"My girlfriend did me a favor," she replied.

"Wow, some favor."

"She's a tall, curvy blonde, definitely a looker."

"She sounds talented," I chortled.

"She told the cops she was from out of state. She spoke with a foreign accent and was asking for their assistance. They obliged. The cops were falling all over her. They followed her everywhere. Marla was dressed in a mini skirt with a very low-cut blouse and was wearing red high heels. She was the bomb. I don't think she was wearing any panties. She had gardenia-scented perfume on which drives men wild," Alison said.

"I get it."

"It worked, didn't it?"

"Most definitely."

"So back to your story about Bravta. Tell me more."

"A couple of weeks ago my brother-in-law, Hershel was found with his brains blown out slumped over in his bedroom. He was a very popular pastor of a large church here in Omaha. The police first thought it was a suicide because they also found a bag of cocaine in his room. It turns out it was a homicide made to look like a suicide. This tragedy was the act of Bravta. It was revenge carried out against me. The detectives found tracks of mud from the outside door in the kitchen leading all the way up the stairs to his bedroom where he was murdered execution-style. The tracks were from a size 14 boot. The police say it was the work of a known Bravta member," I said as my voice waivered with emotion.

"That is so tragic. I'm so sorry for your loss, Louis," Alison said as she snuggled her body closer to mine.

It was suddenly quiet as we both were in deep thought. Then she broke the silence.

"Anything else you want to tell me?"

"Well, a week later as the pastor was delivering the final prayer at Hershel's graveside service, a small group of masked men stormed the crowd firing automatic weapons. The panicked crowd ran in all directions. Sadly, the pastor didn't make it. Bullets tore up his body and he fell backwards onto the coffin which was about to be lowered six feet under. My cousin and her husband hid with me behind some large mausoleums. Fortunately for us, there were undercover cops there who

A Travesty of Justice

returned fire. When the masked men heard police sirens, they ran into the woods at the top of the hill," I said.

"And that was Bravta too?"

"Most definitely. In fact, all of these crimes are connected and lead back to Bravta."

"That's scary."

"You're telling me. You can understand now why the Omaha P.D. has been providing me 24/7 police protection."

"Is there more?"

"Are you kidding? There's plenty more. About six weeks ago my son, daughter-in-law, and two grandchildren came up missing. There were no calls and no explanations."

"You mean they just vanished?"

"They totally vanished. Their table was all set with food and drink. They were prepared to eat and suddenly they vanished. Their car, car keys, their wallet and purse were all left behind. And just a few days ago, their house was demolished by a bomb and a devastating fire. Nothing like covering up evidence. That is a travesty of justice."

"That's so tragic and sad," Alison empathized.

"I couldn't take it anymore, so I even took a cab to Guns Unlimited about a week ago to buy a gun for protection."

"You own a gun?"

"Yes, a .45 automatic," I replied.

"Are you carrying it with you now?" she asked as she ran her hand down my body to my pocket.

"Yes," I squirmed trying to stay calm.

"Oh, let's see what else is down there," she said seductively with a giggle.

"Keep your eyes on the road, Alison. We don't want to get killed," I demanded.

She took her hand off my pocket and placed it on my neck rubbing it in an affectionate manner.

"What happened at the gun store?" she asked.

"On my way to Guns Unlimited there was a jacked-up Tahoe with fancy-wire rims following our cab. There were three men dressed in black in that vehicle. The cab driver patiently waited and was parked outside the gun store with his engine running."

"And what happened next?"

"When I came out of Guns Unlimited with my newly purchased .45 automatic, I noticed that my cab driver had fallen asleep. I walked around to his window and tapped on the window to wake him. He wouldn't wake up, so I opened the driver-side front door and looked closer. He had been shot in the back of the head and was not breathing. There was blood everywhere and all over the back of his seat. I realized someone had killed him."

"Another sign from Bravta?" she asked.

"Yes, a gruesome warning to back off. You see, I had three investigations all going on at once: my attempted murder, Hershel's murder, and the disappearance of my family. Evidently that was too much for Bravta."

"That's frightening."

"You're telling me, Alison. That's why this will probably be the last time you ever see me."

"You're not planning on croaking on me are you?"

"No, what I mean is that I'm moving."

"Moving to where?"

"It's top secret."

"You can't even tell little old me?" she whispered seductively.

"Not really. I swore to the FBI and the Omaha P.D. that I wouldn't tell anyone."

Alison moved closer. Her fingers moved magically all over my body.

"Louis, darling, I don't think you heard me the first time. I will make sweet, delicious love to you the way you like it all night long if you'll tell me, pretty please?"

I, like a fool, gave in to my weakness and desire. I hadn't been with a woman since my marriage to my dear, sweet wife Samantha. I was lonely, and I longed for the soft touch of a woman. I was having one of the best times of my life with Alison. I was totally lost in her.

"Okay, Alison, but only for you," I conceded.

"You're a doll, Louis," she replied as she kept rubbing my neck and back with her magical finger tips.

"They put me in the Witness Protection Program and in a week or so they're moving me to Duckwater, Nevada," I confessed.

"Where is Duckwater?"

"It's a tiny town, so small that if you blink you'll have missed it," I said trying to sound flirtatious.

"So there's nothing to do there?"

"Absolutely nothing to do. It is nowheresville."

"Where will you live?"

"Probably in some rinky-dink, dumpy motel."

"That's terrible Louis. I feel for you."

"But first they've got to kill me off."

"Kill you off?"

"Yeah, they're going to stage my death. They said that before they move me, they're going to fake my death in a horrible accident on Edward Babe Gomez Avenue. They were going to widely publicize it locally and nationally. They want Bravta to believe without a doubt that I died. They're planning on staging graphic photos of my mangled car and my body crushed beyond recognition."

"That's unbelievable."

There was a lull in our conversation as we turned off of Interstate 80 and onto the second exit ramp.

"Are we back in Lincoln again?"

"You've got it," she winked.

"Are we staying at the same place as last time?"

"Nope, I've got a big surprise for you. We're going to live it up first class."

We drove a little further through the business area of city lights and entered the downtown area of Lincoln. Then we pulled into a brightly-lit parking lot. The large red sign on the side of the 10-story hotel said: THE CORNHUSKER MARRIOTT.

"Wow, this is a ritzy place. This must cost a fortune."

"Don't you worry about anything. This one's on me," she said as she pulled out a wad of big bills from her tiny purse.

"Wow, how did you get all that money on a waitress's salary?"

"Let's just say I had a lucky week," she replied.

"Either way, I can't let you pay for this."

"And why not? It's my treat and I'll pay if I want to. Besides, this may be the last time we see each other. So let's live it up in style."

We stepped out of the car and strolled hand-in-hand toward the front entrance as if we were two lovers on their honeymoon. I opened the door for her, and we stepped into a luxury hotel with marble floors and ornate wood. We walked up to the marble-covered front counter where the hotel manager asked for our IDs. Alison insisted on us staying in the 10th floor suite with a king-size bed and a Jacuzzi. We told the manager that we were only staying overnight.

"That will be $522 including tax."

Alison pulled out six one-hundred dollar bills from her swanky designer purse and handed it to the manager.

"Keep the change," she said as she smiled at him.

He handed us the hotel key cards to our tenth-floor suite.

We strolled to the elevator with Alison's head buried into my right shoulder. When we stopped in front of the elevator, she leaned over to me, pressed her body firmly into mine, embraced me, and gave me a long, wet kiss. The elevator door opened and interrupted our embrace.

We took the elevator to the tenth floor and walked a few feet to our suite. Before we could open the door, she slowly lifted her mini skirt to tease me with a peak. Then she beckoned me with her index finger as she unlocked the door with the hotel key.

Before I could say another word, she rushed to the Jacuzzi. Alison threw off her mini skirt, blouse, and shoes. She stepped into the hot Jacuzzi and stood straight up, completely naked.

"Louis, aren't you going to join me? The water is steamy and hot," she said enticingly.

A Travesty of Justice

I didn't stop to think. I tore off my shirt, pants, boxers and shoes. I stepped into the Jacuzzi and sat beside her. We ordered our favorite Chablis from room service. We talked and made love all night. We raised our glasses to us and to the beautiful relationship that we had. We realized that this could be the last time we'd ever see each other again.

CHAPTER NINETEEN

THE SURPRISE ATTACK

It was just another Friday at the Omaha Police Department. Captain Willis and the detectives were in their offices filing reports. It was a quiet day, nothing much was going on in the way of crime. Everyone was ready to check out for the weekend when at precisely 10:21 a.m. all hell broke loose.

A car sped past the front of the downtown police headquarters, and the driver tossed a grenade through one of the front windows of the station. A massive explosion rocked the building and blew out the glass in every window. Smoke was billowing out of the broken windows. A tear gas bomb was lobbed through another window of the station by another driver in a fast-speeding car.

A small army of masked men stormed the front entrance of the police station. They were armed with AK-47's and M-16 automatic rifles. They had caught the officers off guard, shooting to kill everyone in their sight. There was splattered blood on the walls, floor, and ceiling. There were pieces of brain stuck to the walls and bodies of dead officers lying everywhere. The officer at the front desk had the top half of his head shot off and his torso still remained seated in his chair. As the remaining officers in the building realized they were under attack, they returned fire with their weapons but were greatly outnumbered.

Captain Willis frantically reached for his automatic pistol and hid behind his desk waiting for the masked men as they entered each area of the police station and open fired.

"Mayday, mayday. We're under attack. Calling all backup

A Travesty of Justice

with an urgent response to the downtown P.D.," Captain Willis screamed on his radio.

Before Captain Willis could fire his pistol, his body was shredded by several magazines fired directly into his body by five masked gunmen. He never knew what hit him. Pieces of his body were strewn all over his office. His office was splattered with blood from the hundreds of bullets that hit him as well as blood from two other officers who were with him at the time.

The army of masked men had slaughtered every officer in the building, including some of the prisoners in the cells. As the masked men were leaving the front entrance of the station, they were confronted with an army of backup officers and a S.W.A.T. team that open fired on them. They returned fire, but some of their bodies were sprayed with bullets. Realizing that they were trapped in open fire, the masked men ran back into the police station. Realizing they couldn't escape, each one of them detonated a bomb attached to their backpacks. One by one, each masked man blew himself up until there was no one left alive from the attacking army.

The force of the suicide explosions was so powerful that it threw many of the backup officers and S.W.A.T. team members to the ground. Some of their bodies or what was left of their bodies were thrown out of the doors and windows. It was like nothing Omaha had ever seen before. It was a catastrophe.

The entire police station was surrounded by S.W.A.T. team members, backup police officers, fire-fighter crews with their trucks, police cars, and television camera crews.

A television news reporter from KETV 7 was the first to arrive on the scene. She set up with a camera about 50 feet from the demolished police station.

"This is breaking news from KETV 7. We are reporting to you live from downtown Omaha where a devastating tragedy has occurred. Callie Cromwell is standing in front of the main police station. Can you tell us exactly what happened Callie?"

"This is Callie Cromwell reporting live from downtown Omaha. About 10:23 this morning a grenade was hurled through the window of the downtown Omaha Police headquarters. Witnesses say that a tear gas bomb was also thrown into the police station window from a fast-speeding car. There was a loud rumbling explosion that could be felt for several blocks away.

Immediately following the explosion, a man across the street saw what appeared to be a small army of 25 armed masked men storm the front entrance of the downtown Omaha Police headquarters. They were carrying what appeared to be AK-47 and M-16 automatic rifles. He called 911. There appears to be massive casualties. Some are calling this the Omaha Police Massacre," Ms. Cromwell reported.

"Why use the word massacre? The police were armed, weren't they?" the KETV anchor asked.

"Because they were helplessly caught by surprise and didn't have time to protect themselves. An undetermined number of police officers, administrators, and prisoners are believed to be dead," Ms. Cromwell answered.

"Thank you, Callie. We are reporting to you live at the downtown Omaha Police headquarters. We will continue to report any additional breaking news as we learn more about this very tragic story," the KETV anchor said.

The Omaha police draped a yellow DO NOT CROSS tape around the entire building. After it appeared to be safe to enter the building, the FBI, additional S.W.A.T. team members, and Omaha Police detectives swarmed the outside and inside of what was left of the demolished police station. They combed the area for any evidence. They took photos of the bloody crime scene and counted the number of the remains of bodies that littered the offices and hallways of the police station. It was a devastating scene. The sight of their fellow officers' body parts scattered throughout the building meshed in massive amounts of blood was too much for many of the officers investigating. Sure, they had seen many violent crimes before, but this crime was overwhelmingly emotional for them.

CHAPTER TWENTY

THE BACKLASH

"Mr. Green answer this door immediately," the man shouted as he pounded on my hotel door.

I had lain down to rest when I was awaken by the loud pounding on my door. I rolled out of bed and noticed that the clock read 11 a.m. I stepped over to the door and slowly opened it.

"Who is it?" I asked sleepily.

"It's Detective Sully, let me in at once," he demanded.

When I saw who it was, I opened the door to let him in.

"What's going on?"

"Have you heard the news?"

"No, what is going on?" I asked as my words came out drowsily.

"There's been a massive attack on the downtown police headquarters!" he shouted at the top of his voice.

"That's horrible."

"No kidding. Captain Willis was brutally killed and none of the officers or detectives made it out alive," Detective Sully informed me.

"I am so sorry," I replied, not knowing what else to say.

"I'm so angry right now that I can hardly speak," Detective Sully said.

"I am very sorry," I repeated. "What exactly happened?"

"At 10:23 this morning someone lobbed a grenade into the front window of the police station from a passing car. Then someone threw a tear gas bomb into the window from another car. Immediately after that, an army of masked men stormed the front entrance with AK-47's and M-16 assault rifles. They killed everyone in sight. The officers and detectives didn't know what hit them. They didn't have time to defend themselves. When they realized what was happening, the few officers still alive drew their pistols and returned fire. But they were outnumbered. Every one of the officers, detectives, and prisoners is dead. They were slaughtered," Detective Sully said as he held his head between his knees with excruciating pain.

"That is unbelievable," I said as I was trying to find words to console him.

The whole room grew quiet as no one knew the right words to say.

"A video was released a few minutes ago from Bravta claiming responsibility for the attack," Detective Sully finally said.

"Dear God, that is shocking."

"You better believe it. You are in grave danger, Mr. Green. If they can do this to the police station, imagine what they could do to this hotel. They could storm this hotel and kill every one including you. We don't have the man power to adequately protect you anymore."

"What are we going to do?"

"We're going to move you to a secret location here in Omaha while we're waiting to move you to Duckwater."

"I'm ready whenever you are."

"A little while ago on the news, the mayor, local, and state representatives gave angry statements condemning this senseless violence from Bravta," he continued.

"It's definitely a savage act of terrorism."

"Yes, and the public won't stand for it. I can see it now — a total backlash against Bravta."

Detective Sully was right in his assessment of the whole situation. In the days ahead, there were angry letters written to the *Omaha Herald* condemning the brutal attack. The *Omaha Herald* also strongly condemned Bravta in their editorial section.

Council members, legislators, state representatives, and the governor all appeared on television. They called for tough

A Travesty of Justice

measures against Bravta. They urged the citizens of Omaha not to be afraid but to stand strong and courageous. The story was gaining traction in the national media. There were reports about the vicious, cowardly police killings on the television news channels all over the United States. Governor after governor and senator after senator rose to the occasion to condemn Bravta. If Bravta was going to win any public favor, they would have to work hard in their public relations department. They were losing ground fast with the public, yet they had a forcible stronghold in Omaha, the United States, and the world. The public disapproval was not going to stop the over 300,000 Bratva members worldwide from doing their evil acts of crime.

To make matters worse and to aggravate the public after an already damaging public relations fallout, Bravta decided to release bootleg photographs of the police massacred everywhere on social media. Gruesome, graphic scenes of bullet-riddled bodies and blood-covered bodies with organs protruding were tweeted and posted on Facebook. No one knew how Bravta was able to obtain those photographs, but there they were for the whole world to see.

This cowardly tactic only exasperated the public outrage even further. That didn't concern Bravta in the least bit. Bravta was an arrogant, cocky, powerful bunch of thugs and cowards. They did it because they could.

But before any of that happened, Detective Sully and other officers gathered around me in my hotel room trying to decide on a strategy to safely relocate me until I was transported to Duckwater through the Witness Protection Program.

"Okay, Mr. Green, we've checked your room thoroughly. There are no bugs nor any hidden audio-video devices in your room. It is safe to talk," Detective Sully informed me.

I breathed a sigh of relief and asked, "Okay, so what's the plan?"

"Ever heard of the Magnolia Hotel?"

"No, can't say I have."

"It's really nice with five-star service, a Jacuzzi, and they even deliver a hot fresh chocolate chip cookie to your room every night," he said.

"Wow, what a hotel."

"But don't get too used to it. We'll be moving you out of there soon. And the next place will look like a dump compared to this."

"You mean no hot cookies delivered to me before bedtime?" I asked jokingly.

"You know what I mean, Mr. Green. Don't get cute with me."

"Hey, I was only joking."

"We've got the go-ahead from our acting captain. I'll radio ahead to make sure it is safe to move you," Detective Sully said.

"I'm ready when you are."

I had gathered what little I had in clothes and packed them in two large plastic bags. I was ready to go wherever they sent me. My life was in their hands and in God's.

"Okay, Mr. Green, we've got a green light," the detective said.

I was escorted out of my hotel room, down the hallway, into the elevator, and out of the hotel into the parking lot by Detective Sully and a group of ten officers.

At that point, I felt like the President being closely guarded and protected by the world-class Secret Service. Detective Sully opened the back passenger door of his car and seated me in the middle. There was an officer seated on each side of me. There was an officer seated in the front passenger seat and Detective Sully was in the driver's seat. But then I started to feel more like a closely-guarded prisoner than the President of the United States. I felt like a dangerous criminal being transported to a maximum-security prison. There were two police cars in front of our car and two cars behind us. We pulled out of the Days Inn parking lot. It was 10:30 in the morning and the traffic was sparse. We traveled down Main Street and headed to the downtown hotel hoping not to garner much attention. A few people walking along the street stopped and stared at our motorcade of police vehicles.

Finally, our motorcade reached its destination, the Magnolia

A Travesty of Justice

Hotel on Howard Street. We pulled into the loading zone, close to the front entrance. A handful of officers left their cars and searched the entire outside of the hotel and inside of the lobby. When it appeared that it was safe to enter the hotel, Detective Sully and the other officers helped me out of the car. They escorted me through the double glass doors that were so ornately encased with polished brass.

Detective Sully had already prearranged the check-in details with the hotel. There were three officers on both sides of me as Detective Sully led me to the elevator. We took the elevator to the tenth floor and I followed him to my new temporary residence — room 1008. Detective Sully searched the room first and gave the okay sign for me to enter.

"Wow, this is some hotel," I said.

"Courtesy of the Omaha P.D., Mr. Green," Sully said.

"It's got a king-size bed, a sofa, a big screen TV, a kitchen, and a full bathroom with a Jacuzzi," I said admiringly.

"Again, I repeat, don't get too used to it. You're only here for a short while."

"Hey, Detective, at least I can enjoy it while I can," I replied.

"You'll be safe here, at least I think so. Now comes the hard part — the wait," Detective Sully said as he turned to leave.

CHAPTER TWENTY-ONE

THE COUNTERATTACK

It was 4:22 a.m. The sun hadn't even shown it first rays. The FBI agents sat patiently in their cars parked outside the Naughty Girls Club on South 96th Street. Their black, unmarked vehicles were almost camouflaged with the twilight sky. There was no one on the streets as it was a Tuesday morning and ninety-nine percent of the business in this strip club was conducted on Friday and Saturday nights. That was the main reason the agents had chosen Tuesday morning. It was inconspicuous and what they were about to do would be a complete surprise to those inside who they were tracking. Besides, if gunfire did erupt, there would be the least chance of multiple casualties versus gunfire on a Friday or Saturday night.

There were unmarked agent cars and one armored truck parked on the side of the girl's club and in the alley behind the club.

"Timber," the agents heard distinctly from Special Agent-in-Charge, Agent Hollis through their earpieces connected to their radios. Timber was the code word for the green light signal to move into position to launch the attack. The agents jumped out of their vehicles carrying M-16 assault rifles and their automatic weapons. Most were dressed in body armor with helmets except for Special Agent Hollis and a few other agents. An army of at least 30 agents surrounded the club ready to storm the front and back entrances as soon they were given the go-ahead.

All at once, Special Agent Hollis gave the familiar attack hand signal to the armed agents standing outside the front entrance. Two agents kicked the front door open and agents

A Travesty of Justice

swarmed the sparsely-crowded club with their automatic, high-powered weapons pointed, aimed to fire in all directions.

"Don't anybody move! Hands high in the air so I can see them!" Agent Hollis shouted with an authoritative voice.

There were a handful of half-naked women who apparently had been performing lap dances for customers. They were scantily-clad in thongs or G-strings. There were a few waitresses dressed in nothing but strings of beads. A few customers, all male and filled with booze and possibly some illegal substances, sat at the tables. They were totally caught off guard by the FBI raid.

All of them stood in frozen positions with hands held high. Two tall, sturdy men dressed in black suits who were perhaps bouncers or bodyguards, were standing in the right corner of the room. Ignoring the orders of Agent Hollis, they suddenly fired their automatic pistols as they hid behind several sections of walls in the club.

As soon as the bullets started firing, the girls in the club and customers dropped to the floor screaming, trying to take cover from the spray of bullets. The FBI agents took cover behind tables flipped over and returned their fire with their M-16's.

Seeing that they were outnumbered and outgunned, the two bodyguards grabbed what looked like the manager of the club and scurried out the back fire exit.

Agent Hollis and several agents chased them through the exit door as they continued to exchange heavy gunfire. Most of the agents stayed behind to keep watch on the girls and customers they had apprehended. The bodyguards and manager ran down a dark alley behind the night club.

Agent Hollis and the other agents were closing in on them. They continued firing at the escaped assailants. As the assailants reached the end of the alley which intersected Nina Street, they split off in different directions—the bodyguard with the manager ran toward South 96th Street and the other bodyguard ran the opposite direction.

"I've got the lone one, you take the others," Agent Hollis yelled as he ordered the other agents to pursue the bodyguard and manager.

Agent Hollis chased the lone bodyguard across several lawns of houses toward the next street over. The other agents were in pursuit of the bodyguard and manager. They cut across lawns in the opposite directions and continued exchanging gunfire.

The lone bodyguard climbed a tall wooden fence as a vicious Doberman chased him and bit his right foot. Agent Hollis slowed down and immediately froze as the feisty Doberman approached ready to strike him as well.

Agent Hollis quietly radioed the other agents back at the club.

"Damn dog is about to rip my jugular," he said in a state of panic.

"Where's your 10-4?" an agent asked.

"I lost one of them. He jumped the fence and is running back toward South 96th Street," Agent Hollis reported.

Several agents immediately left the night club and began looking for the lone bodyguard escapee.

Meanwhile, Agent Hollis slowly and cautiously backed away from the Doberman who was salivating with his teeth clenched, body leaning forward ready to pounce on the agent. As Agent Hollis backed away a few feet at a time, the Doberman continued to inch forward toward him.

Agent Hollis feared for his life. He could have shot the dog dead with one shot, but he was an adamant animal lover and animal rights advocate. It greatly bothered him if he had to injure or kill any animal — even the Doberman that was about to attack him.

"Good boy, nice boy, I'm not going to hurt you," Agent Hollis said softly with a calming voice to the dog.

Agent Hollis continued to talk softly and sweetly to the dog as he froze like a statue. He slowly lowered his gun so as not to point it at the dog.

After over 30 minutes of softly and calmly talking to the Doberman, the dog's temperament changed. The dog began to calm down and walked up to the Agent Hollis's shoes, sniffed

A Travesty of Justice

them, and then calmly walked away.

"Phew," Agent Hollis said as he let out a long sigh of relief.

Hollis, after realizing the bodyguard was long gone, headed back to the girl's club. He thought all of his troubles were over for now.

"Requesting back-up immediately," a panicked voice came over Agent Hollis's radio.

"What are your coordinates?" Hollis asked.

"We're at 41.22 latitude and -96.06 longitude on the other side of South 97th Street. We've got a hostage situation. Requesting all back-up immediately," the voice said.

Agent Hollis checked the coordinates with his GPS on his phone. The GPS led him through random front and back yards.

What if I run into another Doberman or a German Shepherd? That's all I need right now, Hollis thought to himself as he hurried along toward the hostage situation.

It would be just a little farther according to his GPS. He cut across a driveway and another backyard and suddenly stopped in his tracks. Directly in front of him standing on the front steps of the brick house was the same bodyguard and manager that they had chased earlier through rapid gunfire. Only this time the bodyguard had his gun pointed to the head of an elderly woman in her pajamas with his other hand wrapped tightly around her neck. The manager had his gun pointed at what looked like the elderly woman's husband who was also dressed in pajamas. He had his gun aimed at the back of her husband's skull. The husband was down on his knees screaming and pleading with the gunman not to take their lives.

This was a very tense situation. The two agents who had chased the bodyguard and manager had their weapons pointed at the assailants. The bodyguard and manager were ready to kill the elderly woman and her husband.

And then Agent Hollis arrived to the scene. This would be a dangerous and difficult situation for everyone to escape — particularly alive. Something had to give.

CHAPTER TWENTY-TWO

A BOTCHED OPERATION

"Damn bastards, mother slime scumbags!" Special Agent Hollis shouted in a fit of rage as he threw a glass pitcher of water against the wall and smashed it before the other agents' eyes.

The agents in the aftermath meeting at a secret location in Omaha stared in silent shock as they watched the temper tantrum from their boss.

"Bravta made us look like total idiots," Hollis said as he continued to rant slamming his fist against a nearby table.

"We had reliable intel that said Bravta higher ups would be there," an agent piped up.

"It was bogus intel. Damn weasels weren't there like they were supposed to be when we hit the club," Agent Hollis angrily complained.

"We did our best," another agent said defensively.

"That piece of trash bodyguard got away because of the Doberman who was about to rip my throat out!" Agent Hollis shouted.

"No disrespect boss, but couldn't you have shot him dead?" another agent said.

The room grew quiet as if the agent had said something dreadfully wrong. Agent Hollis looked disgusted after those comments about shooting the dog dead.

"We raided the club and all we could find were a few whores, hookers, two bodyguards, the manager and a few drunk customers. Is that what you call a successful operation?" Agent Hollis asked.

"We shut the place down didn't we?" an agent said proudly.

A Travesty of Justice

The other agents in the room looked down at the floor as if they were shamed by Agent Hollis.

"The most disgusting and embarrassing PR part was the hostage situation which failed miserably," Agent Hollis said.

"All of our men made it, didn't they?" another agent asked.

"All except one. He was killed instantly. Shot in the face when we rushed the bodyguard and manager who were holding the old woman and her husband hostage," Agent Hollis said.

The agents sitting in the room tried their best to be sympathetic and respectful to Agent Hollis.

"It was a tense standoff. Before the other agents and S.W.A.T. team could get there, the old lady and her husband had their brains blown out. The bodyguard and manager felt threatened. They weren't patient enough nor in the mood to negotiate," Agent Hollis said.

Agent Hollis seemed thoroughly disgusted at that point.

"It's inexcusable. It shouldn't have happened that way. We lost one of ours and Bravta lost the bodyguard and manager. It's a damn shame that the old lady and her husband had to be pulled into the middle of that," Agent Hollis said.

Everyone in the room tried to avoid looking at Agent Hollis at that point.

"Gentlemen, I'm afraid that this is just the beginning. We've opened up a large ugly can of worms," he warned.

The agents look startled at the words of warning from Agent Hollis.

"Revenge is coming. This could be all out war," Agent Hollis warned.

CHAPTER TWENTY-THREE

ALL-OUT WAR

Agent Hollis and Detective Sully decided to pay me a visit. They planned on catching me up on all that had been going on between them and Bravta.

It was about 9:05 on Wednesday morning. Agent Hollis and Detective Sully pulled out of the parking lot in their unmarked police car from a secret undisclosed makeshift Omaha P.D. location on the west side of town.

"God, I wish we had never raided the Naughty Girls Club like we did," Agent Hollis said.

"Well you did. What's done is done," Detective Sully replied.

They headed east on Interstate 80 toward downtown Omaha where my hotel was.

Out of nowhere two black Tahoes appeared — one which was riding the bumper of Agent Hollis's car and the other was parallel to their car in the left passing lane.

The back passenger-side window burst into tiny pieces as several bullets ripped through the glass. The bullets came within a few inches of Agent Hollis's earlobe.

"Mother F-----s!" Agent Hollis yelled at the top of his voice.

He pressed his right foot on the gas pedal all the way to the floor as he swerved and sped forward at lightning speeds.

"Bastards! Someone's trying to kill us!"

As Agent Hollis sped up on Interstate 80 the Tahoe with dark-tinted windows caught up with him. A man dressed in black wearing sunglasses protruded out of the front passenger-side window and continued firing bullets.

The other Tahoe caught up with Agent Hollis's car and was ramming the rear bumper forcefully trying to cause Agent Hollis and Detective Sully to crash.

By that point, Detective Sully was beyond pissed. He was boiling over with anger. Sully immediately climbed over the front seat and positioned himself, crouched down on the floor by the rear passenger seat. He aimed his automatic weapon skillfully and carefully at the front tire of the Tahoe where the bullets were being fired.

At the same time bullets were flying from the tailgating, rear-slamming Tahoe, which smashed the rear window of Hollis's car.

Detective Sully's bullets struck the right tire of the Tahoe which was on the left side and parallel to Hollis's car. A loud rushing sound of air being forcefully released from the front tire could be heard. There was a piercing, grinding sound of metal against metal as the Tahoe on the left side veered uncontrollably off to the right and into the direct front pathway of Hollis's car. Hollis continued driving his car at a high rate of speed. All at once, the car Agent Hollis was driving uncontrollably slammed into the side center of the Tahoe, forcing the vehicle to flip over several times. As it finally came to a grinding stop, the Tahoe burst into massive flames. Miraculously, Agent Hollis was able to keep driving his vehicle, but the Tahoe ramming his bumper from behind continued riding his rear end and bullets were being fired from that vehicle.

Detective Sully was an experienced and skilled marksman. He could shoot a flea off of a dog's back at 100 yards away. He continued to return fire from the busted-out rear window until he finally got lucky or his skilled experience paid off. One of Sully's bullets pierced through the eye of the driver of the remaining Tahoe. The driver lost control. A man in the front seat tried desperately to get it under control but couldn't. The fast-speeding Tahoe swerved off to the left and into oncoming traffic on the two lanes of the Interstate going in the opposite direction.

It was a horrible sight to see. The out-of-control Tahoe

suddenly slammed into an 18-wheeler truck traveling at over 70 miles per hour.

There was nothing God and all of his angels could do. There wasn't a prayer on the entire planet that could have saved them.

The professional thugs in the Tahoe who had been railroading Agent Hollis's car bumper were totally mangled beyond recognition by the impact of the 18-wheeler truck. Even the airbags couldn't have saved them.

Despite the fact that Hollis kept driving and that he didn't stop to report the two accidents, he was technically in violation of two hit-and-runs.

But Agent Hollis and Detective Sully were in a big hurry to meet with me in my new hotel. They radioed ahead to report the two devastating accidents to the Omaha P.D.

Agent Hollis and Detective Sully turned off the downtown exit and drove two short blocks to Howard Street. They parked in a no parking zone and placed a sign on the front dashboard that read: OFFICIAL GOVERNMENT BUSINESS.

Both Hollis and Sully had become very paranoid after their recent encounters with Bravta. They were taking extreme measures and precautions to ensure their safety and stay alive. Hollis and Sully stepped out of their vehicle cautiously. They firmly held their automatics in their hands pointing them in various directions as they scouted the area between the curb where they were parked and the Magnolia Hotel front door entrance. Any minute now they could be ambushed by some Bravta members lurking from behind a building.

Agent Hollis and Detective Sully entered the hotel lobby looking over their back and shoulders as they took the elevator to the tenth floor. There was a loud knock on my door. I peeped through the security door hole in the upper center part of the door. Then I slowly and cautiously cracked the door with the security chain still attached.

"It's Agent Hollis and Detective Sully. You can let us in Mr. Green," Hollis said.

I unlatched the security chain and opened the door.

"It's a war zone out there," Detective Sully said.

"So much has happened Mr. Green since we last talked," Agent Hollis added.

Hollis and Sully took a seat across from me by my couch.

"After the police massacre a few days ago, the FBI launched a raid on the Naughty Girls Club on South 96th Street. That was a huge blunder if I say so myself," Agent Hollis said.

I sat there and listened attentively.

"We had some bad intel. We were expecting to bust a large group of top dogs in Bravta but instead found a handful of whores, hookers, and a few wasted customers," Agent Hollis admitted.

"Where were the top dogs who were supposed to be there?" I asked.

"They must have gotten word we were going to bust the joint and split early. The only ones there that were a part of Bravta were the manager and two bodyguards," Agent Hollis said.

"Did they get busted?" I asked.

"When they saw that we were armed FBI crashing their party they started firing and running. After we chased them down a long dark alley, they split up and the one bodyguard got away thanks to a ferocious Doberman who tried to end my life," Agent Hollis said.

"The others weren't so fortunate," Detective Sully added.

"The other bodyguard and the manager both got their brains blown out after they held an old lady and her husband hostage on the front steps of a house off of South 97th Street. It's too bad the old lady and her husband didn't make it either. They were killed instantly by the bodyguard and manager. It was tragic and problematic," Agent Hollis said.

"Sounds like a catastrophe," I said.

"Don't rub it in Mr. Green," Agent Sully replied.

"We've got a full-fledged war going on here. Bravta released a video on YouTube and Twitter which has been carried by all of the media. They declared war against the FBI, Omaha P.D., and the citizens of Omaha," Agent Sully said.

"So what do you plan to do?"

"We're going to give them a war like they've never seen," Agent Sully replied.

"One thing for sure is that it's becoming almost impossible to keep you safe anymore," Agent Hollis said.

"We need to plan your death soon," Agent Sully insisted.

"Plan my death?"

"What I mean, Mr. Green, is that we need to fake your death, get it into the national news, and get you out of town fast before you land in the morgue," Agent Hollis said.

"How soon can you arrange that?"

"We're planning on tomorrow or the next day for your death and your relocation," Agent Hollis replied.

CHAPTER TWENTY-FOUR

GETTING SAFELY OUT OF TOWN

"Are you ready?" the voice on the other end of my cell phone asked.

"Sure am," I replied.

"I'll be there in a few minutes," the voice said.

It was already 6:00 a.m. The sun's orange-color rays were beaming through the partially-cracked drapes in my hotel window. I was so tired of living in Omaha hidden away in hotels. I was exhausted from constantly worrying about being struck down by a bullet from a sniper or being blown up into tiny pieces by a Bravta assassin. I couldn't go anywhere without disguising myself or being escorted by the FBI agents and the Omaha P.D. I was a slave to my surroundings. I was a prisoner trapped in these hotel walls. I was no longer the Louis Green I once was. I had become a withdrawn, fearful, and paranoid man, except for the escapades I had experienced with Alison, my life was no life at all. I longed to return to my farm in Griswold. I missed Norris, Julie, and my grandchildren.

I had rapidly become very fond of my friend, Alison. Every time we had been together it was an adventure of a lifetime. I wished that Alison and I could run away to a far-off, distant place and settle down together. I felt like what we had going in our relationship could really work. I thought about the possibility of Alison and I reconnecting after I got out of the Witness Protection Program—that is if I ever got out of the program. But a quick Google search advised me to never leave the program unless I had a death wish. I faced the fact that I could possibly be enrolled in the Witness Protection Program for the rest of my life. That was a depressing thought. But if I left the program, I would be leaving at my own risk. Even if all of the Bravta members and assassins were killed or put away in prison for life, I could still be writing my death ticket if I chose to leave the program. It would be like me walking around with a bull's eye on my back. Still, it was fun to dream about the day that perhaps Alison and I could live together on my farm in Griswold.

There was a loud knock at the door. I peered through the security glass hole in the door. It was Agent Hollis and two other agents. I opened the door slowly and cautiously to let them in.

"Are you packed and ready?" Agent Hollis asked.

"I'm as ready as ever. I can't wait to get out of this town."

"Careful what you wish for."

I was silent as I stopped and pondered his comment.

"Oh, Mr. Green, these are U.S. Marshals Bailey and Diaz. Since you are now part of the Witness Protection Program, you will no longer be under the watchful eye of the FBI and the Omaha P.D. You will now be protected by the U.S. Marshals Service," Agent Hollis said.

I remained silent and took it all in as I nodded to the Marshals standing in my room.

"Could we all sit down over here by the desk? We've got a lot to cover before we can get you out of here," Agent Hollis said.

The Marshals, Agent Hollis, and I sat by the desk.

"Here is the paper work for you to fill out," Marshal Bailey said as he handed me some forms.

"I have to do paper work?" I grumbled.

"You most certainly do if you're going to be protected by the U.S. Marshal Service. This is a program of the U.S. Government, and we take our program very seriously. We make sure all of the I's are dotted and all of the T's are crossed before we ship you off clear across the other side of the country," Marshal Bailey said.

I took the forms and remained quiet while I read the

A Travesty of Justice

contract.

"So I'm really going to be Jessica Tompkins," I said.

"Yes, she is your new identity," the Marshal replied.

"You mean that really is going to be my new name?" I asked.

"Yes, seriously. Here is your new Social Security card, your new Nevada driver's license and passport," Marshal Bailey said.

My eyes grew wide as I studied my new Social Security card, driver's license and passport.

"Those photos don't look anything like me."

"Precisely. We Photo-shopped the photo of what you will soon look like, Ms. Jessica Tompkins," Marshal Bailey replied.

"Here is your silicone facial mask, wig, and new clothes you will wear as your new identity, Jessica Tompkins," Marshal Diaz said as he handed me a box of the theatrical costume I was to wear.

I stared at the box with the stuff in it: dresses, skirts, pant suits, bras, panties, hose and women's shoes. Here I was getting ready to lose my total identity, and I didn't like it.

First I was a despised man, then I became "America's Hero" and now I'll become a nobody woman.

"You'll have no contact with the outside world—no cell phone, no computers, no Internet, no Facebook, and no landline phones. You won't be able to contact any family members or friends. You will be totally isolated," Marshal Bailey said.

"Will I at least have a T.V.?"

"Yes, we will give you a T.V. so you can at least be entertained."

"What about my son and daughter-in-law? How will I know what's going on with the investigation?"

"We'll stay in close contact and keep you up-to-date on the ongoing investigations of your son and daughter-in-law's disappearance, your brother-in-law's homicide, and your attempted murder investigation," Marshal Bailey said.

"How will you stay in touch if I have no cell phone, computer or landline?"

"We will personally pay you a visit at random times and keep you updated," Marshal Diaz said.

"Oh and if you have any hobbies or subscribe to any organizations, magazines, etc., you can kiss them goodbye. You are Jessica Tompkins now and you will have nothing to do with your previous life," Marshal Bailey said.

I sat there without saying a word and took it all in.

"Do you have any other questions?" Marshal Bailey asked.

"When do we leave?"

"As soon as you fill this paperwork out and we get you looking exactly like the Jessica Tompkins in the ID's."

I took about ten minutes to answer all the questions on the forms. I signed them and handed the forms to Marshal Bailey.

"Now, as soon as we can get your disguise ready, we can make the transfer," Agent Hollis said.

"Okay," I said, "I guess it beats the alternative."

Marshals Bailey and Diaz took the silicone, skin-like, molded mask and fit it carefully over my face. They took time to detail my facial features—eye lashes, wrinkled skin, and soft-looking lips. Next they slowly attached the long brown wig to my head.

"What do you think, Mr. Green?" Marshal Bailey asked.

I stared straight into the mirror and was horrified at what I saw. There was a strange, long-haired looking woman with deep wrinkles staring back at me. I didn't say a word to Marshal Bailey. I kept my comments to myself.

So this is what Jessica Tompkins is supposed to look like.

I excused myself and walked into the bathroom. I closed the door and changed into the clothes the Marshals had provided— a navy blue pants suit, a white blouse, and platform shoes. I opened the bathroom door and stood before the Marshals and Agent Hollis.

"How do I look?" I asked.

They both whistled at me playfully.

"You're looking good girl," Marshal Bailey said.

"You've definitely become Jessica Tompkins," Marshal Diaz said.

"Very believable," Agent Hollis added.

"Have you got everything packed?" Marshal Bailey asked.

"Yes, let's get out of here," I demanded.

"Before we leave, I need your old Social Security card, your Iowa driver's license, your old passport, and your cell phone," Marshal Bailey said.

He waited for me to hand over everything. I gave him everything he requested, but he still asked for more.

"If you have any credit cards, debit cards, check cards, check books, or voter cards, please hand them over now. I looked through my wallet and surrendered everything that had my old name on it.

"Good. Now here is your new credit card and some spending money," Marshal Bailey said.

I took the card and cash and placed them in my nearly-empty wallet. I was all set with my new identity, my new ID's, credit card, and cash.

"Let's go," Marshal Bailey commanded as he closed the hotel room door behind us and led me down the hallway toward the elevator. Agent Hollis and Marshal Diaz followed. When we reached the first floor lobby, four additional U.S. Marshals joined us.

"Here's your airline ticket, Ms. Tompkins," Marshal Bailey said.

"We are headed to Eppley Airfield. We fly out of Omaha in two hours," Marshal Diaz said.

"Well, gentleman, it has been great doing business with you. She's all yours now," Agent Hollis said.

I was quiet and tried to follow instructions as I was very new to the program.

The Marshals escorted me out of the hotel, through the parking lot, and helped me into their black U.S. Government Tahoe. An official Marshal sat on each side of me in the back seat, one sat in the front passenger seat and Marshal Bailey drove. Marshal Diaz and another Marshal followed us in his Tahoe.

It was only a ten-minute drive from the hotel to OMA (Omaha Metropolitan Airport). We made a few turns and ended up on Douglas Street and finally turned on Abbott where the airport was located.

We pulled up in front of the American Airlines sign for departing flights. Marshal Diaz got out of his car from behind. The other Marshals opened the back door and helped me out of the Tahoe. I was escorted through the airport entrance by six Marshals who led me to the security check line. I cleared security and walked to gate B-5 where the Marshals and I would board American flight 492 to Las Vegas, Nevada. There was no major airport close to Duckwater. The closest was Las Vegas, which was about 275 miles away from Duckwater.

Finally, after waiting for over 30 minutes, an American Airlines representative called for us to board. We walked the long ramp, entered the plane, and sat in rows A1 through A6 in the front of the plane. Then the flight attendants locked the doors of the plane. As the plane was backing up and starting to taxi down the runway toward take-off, I suddenly felt a reservoir of emotions rise and overcome me. These were deep-seated emotions that I must have hidden for a very long time. I felt homesick. I missed Griswold. I felt sad and lonely knowing I had left Louis Green behind in Omaha. I missed my son and daughter-in-law and my grandchildren. I was about to start a whole new life as Jessica Tompkins and about to leave all of my memories behind me. Somehow it didn't quite seem fair. But I pulled myself together because I really had no choice in the matter — either I cooperated or I would end up in a pine box somewhere in a funeral home.

I decided to relax and found myself dosing off in complete exhaustion. I must have slept for over an hour because when I woke up I heard the flight attendant ask us to put our trays in the upright position and to make sure we had our seatbelts fastened as we were preparing to land in Las Vegas. I could feel the plane descend and could see the tall buildings of Vegas outside my window. I heard the landing gear open and the wheels descend. Finally, I felt the wheels touch the runway as the brakes worked overtime to slow the plane down to a halt.

The flight attendant on the microphone asked that all

A Travesty of Justice

passengers remain seated until we left the plane. The six Marshals and I rose from our seats and left the plane through the connecting ramp. Instead of taking the usual route that led to the terminal, we took a side exit door with stairs that led to the lot of the terminal. Four black Tahoes were parked beside the planes. Marshal Bailey and the other Marshals helped me into the first Tahoe that was waiting. The other Marshals entered the vehicle. There were three additional Tahoes behind our car.

Marshal Bailey set his GPS in the vehicle.

"Duckwater is about 275 miles from here, Ms. Tompkins," Marshal Bailey said.

"Are you talking to me?" I asked.

"Yes, and you better start getting used to your new name."

Marshal Bailey started the engine and put the Tahoe in drive. Our vehicle and the three other Tahoes headed out toward the highway that led to my new permanent residence, Duckwater. As we drove to the end of Las Vegas, the sun was beginning to set. The barren desert surrounding the highway looked eerie.

To think I'm going to be living in this hellhole of all places.

Everyone in the car hadn't said a word since we left Vegas. They must've been tired or bored.

How am I going to pass the time with no cell phone, computer, landline, or friends?

The sun was going down rapidly. We still had another hour to go according to the highway signs. It would be dark by the time we reached Duckwater.

Duckwater, who the hell came up with a name like that?

I started humming to myself because boredom had already set in.

I see why there are only 334 people living in Duckwater. Who the hell would want to live there?

"It's really cold tonight, about 15 degrees. We just might get some snow," one of the Marshals said as he was trying to break the silence with some small talk.

"Looks like a full moon too," another Marshal said.

I kept quiet because I was in no mood to talk or be jolly. I was being committed to a hellhole prison out in the middle of nowhere, and I was in a foul mood.

We continued driving on U.S. Route 93 North. I noticed that we were climbing in altitude as I spotted the desert mountains all around us.

Later we turned left onto Nevada State Highway 318 and then onto U.S. Route 6 and finally right onto Route 379. It was such a long trip. I was ready to bust out of that vehicle.

"I haven't heard much from you lately," Marshal Bailey said.

"I'm alright," I replied.

I did a good job of lying. If he really knew how I felt, he would've told me to go screw myself.

I couldn't believe my eyes. There was the WELCOME TO DUCKWATER sign on the Great Basin Highway. Our headlights lit up another sign that said we were about to enter the Great Basin National Park. Some of the mountains looked more like rocky ridges and others looked like jagged mountains that pointed straight toward the sky. The moonlight was very bright and lit up the scenic view of the mountains. It was a strange sight to my eyes as I had never set foot in Nevada in my entire life.

We turned left onto Meadow Road. It was nearly pitch black as it was late when we arrived. There were only a few lights on in that sleepy town. There were no cars on the road. It was just as I imagined it to be — one boring town.

"By the way, Ms. Tompkins, did I mention that there are no motels or hotels in Duckwater?" Marshal Bailey asked.

I was silent and didn't reply.

He led me to believe that I'd be staying in a motel.

"Where will I be staying, a bed and breakfast?"

"Ha, ha, very funny Ms. Tompkins, there are no B and B's around this remote part of Nevada."

I was silent again as I came to a fork in the road. We veered off to the right onto a remote part of Sugar Shack Road. Then we turned left onto a rough dirt road where we traveled for about a quarter of a mile off of the paved road. The headlights

A Travesty of Justice

of the Tahoe revealed a rustic old cabin out in the middle of nowhere. Our car stopped and the Marshals helped me out of the back seat.

"This is it, your new residence," Marshal Bailey said.

My eyes stared at the rough, crude cabin where I was about to set up residence. I didn't say a word.

"It's rather primitive. It has running water, a bed, a satellite T.V. and a kitchen stocked with food," Marshal Bailey said.

"Courtesy of the U.S. Government," Marshal Diaz said.

"At least you'll be safe here," said Marshal Bailey. "But there are no guarantees."

CHAPTER TWENTY-FIVE

CONSCIOUS OF MY OWN DEATH

I was over 1,000 miles away in Duckwater, Nevada, and they were already executing my tragic death in Omaha, Nebraska. It was a cloudy and dreary day in Duckwater. While I was sitting in my rustic, primitive one-bedroom cabin eating pancakes and bacon for breakfast, a fatal, scandalous one-car accident occurred at precisely 8:02 a.m. on that cold Friday, January 29.

It was conveniently snowing that morning and the roads were slick as the temperatures had fallen to a low of 9 degrees. The whole accident was so suspicious that it's a wonder anyone fell for it—particularly Bravta.

I was supposedly riding in a cab heading to the airport. My cab was traveling near the Southroads (in the South Omaha area of town) on the windy Edward Babe Gomez Avenue. The road was considered dangerous and not well maintained. It was almost always deserted. When you added snow to a road that was neglected in maintenance, you got a perfect setting for a fatal accident. My cab was said to be traveling at a high speed of 82 miles an hour which is considered reckless driving inside the city of Omaha. They said I was running late and trying to board a plane to Los Angeles. I guess they used the perfect excuse since that was the place I was left for dead when I was shot in the head after appearing on the *After Hours Show*.

Supposedly, my cab driver lost control of the vehicle when it veered suddenly to the right of the sharp curve on that two-lane road. According to the news reports, he had overcorrected his cab and had hit a guard rail, which caused his cab to flip over a short embankment. The cab rolled three times before it landed

A Travesty of Justice

two feet from the railroad tracks. Apparently, the vehicle had leaked gasoline before the driver or I could escape. The mangled cab exploded into a ball of flames instantly killing the cab driver and me. The T.V. news channels reported that both our bodies were totally charred beyond recognition. That was so convenient for the FBI and the Omaha P.D. First they bought a used yellow taxi with no title. They registered the title in the cab driver's name. Then they created a fictitious cab driver's name with a fake ID and Social Security number. The news reported his name as Monty Hall. Monty was probably a corpse of a homeless victim found frozen to death one day on a downtown Omaha street. My supposedly mangled and charred body was probably another corpse of a homeless victim.

Something else that the news media did not know was that the FBI had hired two professional stunt men to pull off the amazing feat. They had propped two corpses into the back seat of the yellow taxi. Although the road was almost always deserted, they had professional scouts positioned in both directions of the road to warn the stunt men if anyone were to travel that road. Then the stunt driver jumped into the taxi. The driver started at the south end of Edward Babe Gomez Avenue and pressed the gas pedal all the way to the floor. The driver knew how to drive the taxi in such a way that when he hit the icy stretch of that almost 90-degree curve in that windy road he would hit the guard rail and cause the vehicle to flip. At the same time the taxi hit the guard and started to flip, the stunt driver opened the front driver's side of the vehicle and jumped out. He was dressed in a helmet and heavy-padded suit to minimize any damage to his body. When he jumped out at that precise time at such a high speed, his body literally rolled to a stop on the payment. As the car hit the guard rail and flipped several times to its resting place next to the railroad tracks, both stunt drivers ran down the embankment toward the taxi. Lucky for them the mangled vehicle had not exploded. Both stunt men were able to pry the front passenger door open and drag one of the corpses into the front driver's seat. He was able to place the seatbelt over the corpse to appear as if the driver of the taxi was wearing his seatbelt at the time of the accident. Then the other stunt man placed a seat belt around the other corpse in the back seat. That corpse would have been me, Louis Green (my old identity). My "corpse" was hanging sideways and upside down from the seat belt which held my "body" in as the cab had been turned partially upside down when it landed from being flipped several times.

After the corpses were positioned in such a way that they were locked into their seats with the seatbelts, the stunt men cut the fuel line under the cab. Gasoline started seeping out of the line and finally the stunt men ignited the gasoline with a cigarette lighter. The cab lit up in massive flames as the stunt men ran for the road where the accident had occurred. Before they could join the scouts at the end of the north end of the road, the cab blew up into a large ball of flames. The fire ball could be seen in many parts of South Omaha. There must have been a thousand people who had called 911 that morning about the loud, visible explosion. Meanwhile, the stunt men hired by the FBI were long gone and were headed out of town and possibly out of state. They had disappeared.

It wasn't long before the news had rapidly spread to the Omaha T.V. stations and quickly made its way to the national news.

"America's Hero, Louis Green killed in auto accident this morning," reported WOWT TV News Channel 6 in Omaha.

"America's most-loved hero died from multiple injuries in a single-car crash," said KMTV Action News 3 TV in Omaha.

"A tragic car wreck took the life of America's Hero, Louis Green, in Omaha, Nebraska," A CNN News reporter declared.

"Beloved America's Hero, Louis Green, was unexpectedly killed in a tragic car accident this morning in Omaha, Nebraska," a Fox News reporter said.

My tragic death was now the subject of every conversation during that day and at dinnertime that evening. Every story reported my heroic actions in foiling the Bank of Omaha heist and hostage takeover. They covered my guest appearance on NBC TV's late night show, the *After Hours Show*, and how I had miraculously recovered from being left for dead when someone shot me in the head in December when I was leaving the *After Hours Show*. The news stations seemed to be obsessed with my sudden death. They were fixated on it for days and interviewed residents in Omaha and Griswold.

"I am shocked to learn the news of Mr. Green's sudden death. I worked with Louis in the factory years ago. He was a good man," a Griswold resident said on the evening news.

"This is a sad and tragic day for the town of Griswold. Louis Green was a great man. He was 'America's Hero' and he left a lot of greatness behind him," Griswold's Mayor Bradley said on the news.

I couldn't believe that the Mayor of Griswold had ordered the flags in Griswold to be lowered to half-mast. A few days later the Mayor signed a declaration honoring me with a special day for the citizens of Griswold. That was an unbelievable act of kindness. While I was basking in all of the glory of being honored and remembered, something didn't feel right in my conscious. It was very wrong to make people think Louis Green was dead. While the citizens of Griswold were mourning, I was perfectly alive secluded in a cabin over 1,000 miles away. I wanted to shout to the world and let them know that I was alive. I was ashamed of the scam I was perpetrating. I felt like a total fraud. I didn't feel worthy of the title "America's Hero" anymore. But there wasn't anything I could do about it. I was totally helpless. I became a pawn of the U.S. Marshals Service when I signed up for the Witness Protection Program. It was a sham in some ways, but what other choices did I have? I watched many of the news channels that showed people from all over mourning my death. I felt sad and lonely—totally isolated.

I waited for a public reaction to Louis Green's death from Bravta. But there was none. Surely, they had heard the news by now. I wondered what was going on inside their network to the reaction to the news. There was nothing but silence. Perhaps it was a publicity stunt to remain quiet. Perhaps they were trying to play it cool and look like they were never involved in trying to kill me or any of my family members. But it was perplexing. I am sure it was to the FBI, the Omaha P.D., and to the U.S. Marshals Service as well. I am sure they were expecting a big reaction and confirmation that they had learned of my accidental death. The curiosity was killing me. In fact, Bravta was laying low. There hadn't been a single incident or act of violence in over a week in Omaha. Was the war over? Or was Bravta laying low for public relation reasons? Perhaps they were trying to gain favorability in the public's eyes again. Or maybe this was the quiet before the storm. I pondered all of those questions as I had a lot of time on my hands. I was rotting in sheer boredom.

Surely Bravta was going to make a move soon and it would catch us all off guard.

It didn't really matter. I was hidden away in the secluded town of Duckwater. They couldn't find me on the map if they tried.

CHAPTER TWENTY-SIX

DO AS THE DUCKWATERIANS DO

A few days later I was so bored that I couldn't stand myself being locked up in that musty old cabin of mine. I decided to try out my new identity and spend the day with the town folks in Duckwater.

"I'm Jessica Tompkins. I was born in Petersburg, Alaska. Most of my family is dead. My friends are all gone. I am a retired teacher. I used to teach fourth grade. My husband died five years ago. I moved to the quiet town of Duckwater for peace of mind," I said to myself as I practiced reciting information about my new identity.

I looked over my new ID's, passport, and credit card. I was trying to get familiar with my new self before I met anyone. I was trying to get used to my long brown hair and feminine facial features. I certainly had more wrinkles than I would ever have imagined.

I was ready to venture out into the town in the 2007 Chevy Silverado truck, courtesy of the U.S. Government. I couldn't go very far as the U.S. Marshals Service had a tracking device on the vehicle and knew every move I made.

I showered and got dressed in the same white blouse and navy blue pants suit the U.S. Marshals Service had provided. It was tricky showering with my mask on. I had to avoid washing the mask on my face as it was unmovable. I could remove my wig but the mask had to stay on my face. I placed the long brown wig carefully over my head and grabbed my purse and watch. I put on a dark heavy coat as it was 29 degrees that day. I slowly opened the door and looked around every direction. The sky was cloudy and there was a light wind. I stepped off the porch and into the black Silverado. I started the engine and put it into reverse to back up and turn around. I drove down the rough dirt driveway and turned left onto Sugar Shack Road. I drove on Sugar Shack until I reached Duckwater Falls Road. I turned left onto Duckwater Falls and then a quick right onto the same road. I decided I would hang out at the local U.S. Post Office. I had always heard that the post office was the place you could meet folks and find out all the gossip of a small town.

I parked my Silverado at the Duckwater U.S. Post Office. There were a few trucks and cars parked in front of the building. The Post Office was very plain. It was made of concrete cinder blocks and had a brown-trimmed metal skirt around the front of the building with a flat roof. It resembled a large double wide mobile home. I entered the building through light brown-trimmed, double glass doors. Inside there were a few customers in line for the one window with one postal clerk serving them. I observed how friendly everyone was. They smiled at each other and called everyone by their first names. I was standing around the foyer of the post office near the mailboxes, trying to work up the nerve to get in line to buy a few stamps. But before I could get in line, I struck up a conversation with a man who was getting his mail in the locked mailboxes. He was tall, dark-skinned with coal-black, long-braided beaded hair. He wore a decorative leather coat with colorful markings all over the jacket. I smiled at him and he returned the smile.

"Hi, I'm Jessica."

"I'm Joe."

He knew that I wasn't from around here. I looked different and I spoke differently than the others.

"Are you visiting?"

"No, I live here now," I replied.

"Where you from?"

"I am from Petersburg, Alaska," I replied.

"What brings you here?"

"I'm a retired teacher."

A Travesty of Justice

"And you decided to move to Duckwater?" he asked looking puzzled.

"It's a quiet town and gives me peace of mind."

"It's one of Nevada's ghost towns. We've lost population from 388 to only 334 according to last year's census."

"Where in Duckwater do you live?" I asked.

"I live up the road at the reservation."

"What do you do?"

"I do clerical work for the Duckwater Shoshone Tribal Offices," Joe replied.

"Is there anything I should know about the town?"

"There are three main roads: Sugar Shack, Duckwater Falls, and Meadows Road. There are no stores or gas stations. You have to drive to the big town Elko, which is 40 miles away to find those things," Joe replied.

"What do people do around here for work?"

"Oil drilling, the oil refinery, or ranching."

"How can I meet some of the town folks?"

"Hang out here or get a job in drilling," Joe laughed.

I was lonely and isolated, and I wanted to get to know some of the people in Duckwater. I wanted to learn their ways. I was now a resident of Duckwater, and I wanted to do as the Duckwaterians did.

"Good to meet you, Joe," I said as I left the post office. I had forgotten to buy my stamps. I didn't need them anyway. Who was I going to write to? I didn't have any bills and no associations with anyone. I was Jessica Tompkins. And I had to accept that.

CHAPTER TWENTY-SEVEN

TRAPPED

Another ho-hum week in Duckwater had passed. I was getting comfortable but very bored hibernating in my secluded rustic cabin out in the middle of nowhere. Friday's mountain sunrise had arrived, and I had absolutely nothing to do. I fixed an egg and bacon biscuit in the microwave and downed it with a cup of black coffee. I showered and put my clothes on.

I had heard about the town of Elko with a population the size of almost 20,000 people. Since I got here, I had a burning desire to visit Elko. So I decided to venture out to the town.

"What do I have to lose? It's not that far and things seemed to have calmed down with Bravta," I convinced myself.

I put my heavy coat on, stepped out onto the porch of my cabin, closed the door behind me, and hopped into my Silverado. I started the engine, put it into drive and headed down the quarter-mile, rough, dirt driveway. I turned right on Sugar Shack Road, and turned left on Meadow Road which led me to Highway 379 South. I took Highway 379 for about 20 miles until I reached the town of Currant where Highway 379 and U.S. Highway 6 intersect. I turned left and headed north on Highway 6. Highway 6 north (the Grand Army of the Republic Highway as they called it) took me straight into Elko. It was a mountainous, rough desert terrain that I had to travel. I started to climb elevation as I reached the Humboldt-Toiyabe National Forest. The sun's glorious orange-yellow rays were picturesque as they highlighted the tall Currant Mountain. The highway sign said the elevation of the mountain was 11,513 feet above sea level. The two-lane highway was desolate. I hadn't seen a

A Travesty of Justice

car or a person on the road for miles.

As I continued to drive north toward Elko I thought I was hallucinating or had seen a mirage. Up ahead standing in the middle of the road was what appeared to be a woman waving her hands. As I approached her, she appeared to be in a sheer state of panic. There was a car precariously parked on the side of the road. It appeared to have broken down. I pulled my Silverado off to the side of the road right behind her car. I opened my truck door and ran over to assist her.

"Ma'am, can I help you?" I asked.

Through her extraordinary beauty she was crying. She was in a state of panic.

"My car won't start. The engine light came on a while ago," she explained.

I walked over to the hood of what appeared to be a 2009 Ford Fusion. I lifted the hood and looked around to see what the trouble could be.

Before I could say anything to her, I felt a burlap bag being thrown over my head and a rope tied around my neck. I felt several strong hands grab my arms and body from behind. I couldn't see a thing. I could barely breathe.

"Help, help, let go of me you bastards!" I shouted.

I resisted them by trying to break free. But it seemed like I was outnumbered by too many strong arms. I heard a voice speaking to me. I felt the nozzle of a gun pushed up against the back of my skull.

"Shut the f--k up! I'll kill you right here if you say another word!" the deep voice shouted.

Several strong arms continued to hold my arms still. I felt my body lift off the pavement as I was being carried by what felt like several people. I heard them speaking to one another.

"Get him in there quickly. We've got to get out of here before someone sees us," another voice said.

I heard what sounded like the trunk of a car being opened. Before I could fight back, my entire body was thrown inside the trunk. I heard the lid of the trunk close leaving me in darkness. I gasped to take a breath but had trouble inhaling.

Then I heard several men speaking.

"Put the truck in neutral," one voice said.

It turns out my kidnappers pushed my Silverado off an embankment some 7,000 feet up. They stood and watched as my truck rolled off the side of the highway and flew down the mountainside to its final resting place thousands of feet below. I hadn't heard any explosion. The Silverado miraculously crashed at the bottom of the mountain without exploding into a ball of flames. They wanted to make sure that my truck wouldn't be discovered.

Then I heard the car engine start. I was moving and traveling to an unknown destination.

"Dear Jesus, please help me. Help me get out alive," I quietly whispered to myself.

I felt totally helpless. I didn't know what would happen next. I was beyond scared.

The kidnappers drove their car with me in the trunk for what seemed like hours. I had to go to the bathroom, and I ended up peeing on myself. My throat was dry. My body thirsted for water.

What am I going to do? I'm going to die.

It was the longest nightmare of my life. My body was crawling with fear as I was claustrophobic and went totally berserk being cooped up in a trunk for endless hours. My face was gagged with duct tape wrapped around my mouth. And my hands and feet were bound with rope.

Finally, after agonizing hours of being bound, gagged, and cooped up inside a trunk the size of large suitcase, I heard the car come to a long stop. I could hear people talking and suddenly the trunk popped open. I could feel muscular arms lifting me out of the trunk and carrying me. I could detect that it was still daylight as a tiny bit of light made its way through the burlap bag that covered my face. My body was carried a short distance and I could hear a door open. Whatever building they had just carried me into had a strange echo. Every word the kidnappers said reverberated throughout the building. I guessed I was in a large building with possibly high ceilings

A Travesty of Justice

and wood, tile, or cement floors. They turned my bound and gagged body upright and placed me into a chair. I was finally able to sit in the upright position after being stuffed in a tiny truck for endless hours.

"Would you like something to drink, Mr. Green?" a voice asked.

"Yes," I said with a tired shallow voice.

"I can't hear you, Mr. Green," the voice replied.

"Yes," I said louder as I nodded my head.

Then I could feel arms and hands untying the rope around my neck. As they lifted the burlap bag from my head and face, I started to focus my eyes to the light in the room as it had been dark for many hours. The view around me was blurry as I tried to focus my eyes. Several strong hands ripped the wig and mask from my body. They ripped the duct tape from my mouth as I painfully screamed. I could see a woman with long hair dressed in black walking toward me. It looked like she was holding a glass in her hands. As she started moving closer, my eyes thought they were seeing things. I was shocked beyond belief.

Was I hallucinating from hours of being locked in a trunk?

"Here's your water," she said as she poured the cool liquid into my mouth.

It was the best water I had ever had. I was literally dehydrated at that point and any liquid would have quenched my thirst.

I was totally speechless.

How could this be? She was my friend and lover.

I closed my eyes hoping that it was only a dream. I opened my eyes again and there she was.

I trusted her. She was my friend.

"Aren't you going to say anything?" she asked.

I didn't say a word but anger suddenly boiled inside of me. Without thinking I spat a wad of spit from my mouth which landed on her face.

"You bitch, you mother of all betrayers, you rat, you lowlife scumbag!" I shouted angrily at her.

"Are you finished?" she asked calmly as she wiped my

saliva from her face.

"No, I'm not finished. You used me and made me think we had something special as friends and lovers!" I shouted.

She laughed like a psycho and kept staring at me with her evil eyes. There was what looked like a whole army of heavily-armed men dressed in black that stood all around me in that warehouse.

"You couldn't have possibly believed that a young beautiful woman like me would fall for an ugly old man like you?" she said with a devious voice.

"You're despicable Alison, if Alison is your real name," I replied. "You made me think you had an ordinary waitress job and that you were struggling to make an honest living. But, look at you, you're a lowlife, scumbag bitch who works for Bravta!" I shouted.

"That's enough, Louis," she said.

It was quiet for about 20 seconds.

"I've got a surprise for you," she said teasingly.

I took a few deep breaths and tried to gain my composure after shouting at her with deep-seated anger.

"Bring them out boys," she commanded.

At a distance I could see several tall, muscular men dressed in black carrying what looked like bodies sitting upright in chairs. The four bodies were bound and gagged. Their bodies were tied to the chairs. The kidnappers lined their bodies and chairs up in a straight-line only a few feet from where I was bound and gagged in my chair.

"Are you ready?" a man asked me.

"Ready for what. What the hell are you talking about?" I asked.

Then the tall, muscular men untied the ropes around the four bodies and lifted the burlap bags from their heads and faces.

"Louis Green meet Norris, Julie, Michael and Sadie," one of the men said.

I was flabbergasted. My eyes couldn't believe what I was seeing. I was totally speechless.

A Travesty of Justice

"Is this what you've been looking for?" the man asked, playing psychological games with me.

Norris, Julie, Michael and Sadie couldn't say a word as their mouths were gagged and sealed with duct tape. But their eyes were a dead giveaway. Sheer terror came from their eyes and faces.

"You bastards, you low life, filthy scum of the Earth!" I shouted angrily at them.

"Now, calm down, Mr. Green. There's nothing you can do about it. I've got an army of men armed with M-16's and AK-47's. They're not going anywhere," the man said.

Then a tall, well-built, and dark-haired man stepped forward and stood before me. He appeared as though he might be the leader by the important way he carried himself.

"I'm Sergio. Welcome to our place. We've got big plans for you and your family, Mr. Green," he said.

He held out his hand to shake mine. But again, that was a psychological game as my hands were completely tied behind my back.

"Ever heard of a human shield?" he asked.

"Yes," I replied.

"You and your family have the distinct honor of becoming human shields for our next project," he said with a serious tone in his voice.

I didn't say a word but just listened in silence.

"Next Friday, February 11, the city of Los Angeles will no longer exist. It will be a pile of rubbish contaminated by deadly radiation unless the U.S. Government gives us what we demand—100 million dollars," Sergio said as if he meant every word.

I remained quiet and listened.

"Every heard of the MK54 Backpack Nuke?" he asked.

I shook my head as if I didn't know.

"Only the U.S. and Russia have them. Ours are Russian made. They come from Mexico through the border. Each one weighs almost 100 pounds and can deliver five kilotons of nuclear explosive power. They are carried in a backpack—very heavy. Don't worry, we'll give your grandchildren light-weight ones," Sergio said.

I couldn't believe what I was hearing. I was horrified. We were going to be used as human pawns.

"We will give you a lift to the city and drop you off in five different locations: The Staples Center, the U.S. Bank Tower, The Aon Center, the Braly Building and Two California Plaza. Each nuke bomb will be remotely controlled wirelessly by us," Serio said.

I was beyond scared and terrified. I felt helpless and angry at the same time realizing my family, I, and everyone in Los Angeles would have to die in such a gruesome way.

"L.A. has never experienced such catastrophic explosions. It's no telling what it could do—earthquakes, waves of panic, massive deaths from the radiation, and possibly the total destruction of California," Sergio said.

I couldn't take it anymore. I was furious and terrorized at the same time.

"You'll never get away with it!" I shouted angrily.

"Oh, I think the Feds will come to their senses and give us our money," Sergio replied.

"Never!" I shouted.

"That's where you and your family come in. You are the insurance policy," Sergio said.

"Bastards!" I shouted as I angrily spat a wad of saliva at him.

The large wad of saliva landed near Sergio's left eye. It was obvious he was becoming angry.

"Take him away," Sergio commanded.

Several tall, muscular men grabbed my body tied to the chair and lifted me off of the floor.

"Wait, don't do this to me!" I screamed at the top of my voice.

They carried me into a very dark room and locked the door. It was quiet and still.

Were they going to leave me here to die?

I prayed to Jesus for help. I was a helpless, desperate man.

A Travesty of Justice

CHAPTER TWENTY-EIGHT

THE VISION

I had passed out for some time—too weak from not eating or drinking. I had been in this dark, lonely, isolated room for what seemed like endless hours. I was still bound, gagged, and tied to my chair. No one bothered to check on me.

I was suddenly startled by a blinding bright light that filled the entire room. I thought I was hallucinating or dreaming.

A tall woman dressed in white with large feathered wings appeared and was standing before me. I recognized the woman as the angel who had visited me on a number of occasions. In fact, she resembled the woman who rescued me from the Bank of Omaha robbery-hostage takeover back in December.

"Do not be afraid, Louis. This is a travesty of justice. Help is on the way," she said in a very calm and peaceful voice.

She continued to repeat those words over and over until she faded into the dark. The bright light grew dim until there was total darkness.

-TO BE CONTINUED

ABOUT THE AUTHOR

THORNTON CLINE has been honored with Songwriter of the Year twice in a row by the Tennessee Songwriters Association for his hit song, "Love is the Reason" recorded by Engelbert Humperdinck and Gloria Gaynor. He has received Dove and Grammy nominations for his songs. His articles have appeared in numerous national magazines, newspapers and journals. *A Travesty of Justice* is Cline's tenth published book. He is author of *Band of Angels*, *Practice Personalities: What's Your Type?*, *Practice Personalities for Adults*, *The Amazing Incredible Shrinking Violin*, *The Amazing Incredible Shrinking Piano*, *The Amazing Incredible Shrinking Guitar*, *The Contrary, Not My Time to Go*, and *The Amazing Magical Musical Plants*. Cline is an in-demand speaker for national conferences, workshops, and libraries. Cline lives in Hendersonville, Tennessee, with his wife.

PREVIEW

NO SWEETER JUSTICE is the follow up novel to *A TRAVESTY OF JUSTICE*. Here is an excerpt from chapter one of the new soon-to-be released third book in the series.

MONDAY, FEBRUARY 11, 2010 4:55 A.M.
WAREHOUSE ON RUSSELL ROAD
LAS VEGAS, NEVADA

"Hold your fire until I give the green light," the voice commanded on the two-way radio.

It was 4:55 a.m. and twilight had still graced the Monday morning daylight.

An army of heavily armed S.W.A.T. team militia, FBI agents, Las Vegas Police officers, and National Guardsmen surrounded the old abandoned warehouse on Russell Road in Las Vegas.

"Are you positive they're in there?" another voice asked on the radio.

"Absolutely, 100% positive," a voice replied.

It was quiet and still in the twilight.

"Remember this is our surprise. We're going to eliminate them without killing Mr. Green and his family members," the voice said on the radio.

"That's a roger," one voice said on the two-way radio.

"Roger," another said.

"Got it," another replied.

It was now 5:04 a.m. The sun was starting to show its orange and yellow rays.

There was complete silence except for a distant train sound crossing the tracks.

"Greenlight," said a loud and certain voice.

The FBI agents, SWAT team militia, police, and national guard kicked down the doors of the back and front of the warehouse. They stormed the building and were greeted with heavy gunfire in all directions.

-TO BE CONTINUED-

Purchase other Black Rose Writing titles at www.blackrosewriting.com/books
and use promo code PRINT to receive a 20% discount.

BLACK ROSE writing™